Here Come the Brides

**An exciting trilogy about triplet sisters
separated at birth—but reunited by love!**

MILLIONAIRE TAKES A BRIDE by Pamela Toth
Special Edition #1353 On sale October 2000

When charming rogue Ryan Noble set his mind
on taking a bride, he did just that. Trouble was, he
claimed Sarah Daniels…the wrong triplet! To make
matters worse, his *un*intended bride's irresistible allure
was stealing *his* heart.

THE BRIDAL QUEST by Jennifer Mikels
Special Edition #1360 On sale November 2000

Runaway heiress Jessica Walker went into
hiding as a nanny for handsome Sam Dawson's
darling daughters. But could the sheriff's
little matchmakers convince Jessica that their
daddy was the husband she'd always longed for?

EXPECTANT BRIDE-TO-BE by Nikki Benjamin
Special Edition #1368 On sale December 2000

Pregnant and alone after an unexpected night
of passion with her childhood sweetheart,
Jack Randall, Abby Summers resigned herself
to single-motherhood. Jack had other ideas—he
wanted to make Abby his wife, and he wouldn't take
no for an answer.…

Dear Reader,

The most wonderful time of the year just got better! These six captivating romances from Special Edition are sure to brighten your holidays.

Reader favorite Sherryl Woods is back by popular demand with the latest addition to her series AND BABY MAKES THREE: THE DELACOURTS OF TEXAS. In *The Delacourt Scandal*, a curious reporter seeking revenge unexpectedly finds love.

And just in time for the holidays, Lisa Jackson kicks off her exciting new miniseries THE McCAFFERTYS with *The McCaffertys: Thorne*, where a hero's investigation takes an interesting turn when he finds himself face-to-face with his ex-lover. Unwrap the next book in A RANCHING FAMILY, a special gift this month from Victoria Pade. In *The Cowboy's Gift-Wrapped Bride*, a Wyoming rancher is startled not only by his undeniable attraction to an amnesiac beauty he found in a blizzard, but also by the tantalizing secrets she reveals as she regains her memory.

And in RUMOR HAS IT…, a couple separated by tragedy in the past finally has a chance for love in Penny Richards's compelling romance, *Lara's Lover*. The holiday cheer continues with Allison Leigh's emotional tale of a runaway American heiress who becomes a *Mother in a Moment* after she agrees to be nanny to a passel of tots.

And silver wedding bells are ringing as Nikki Benjamin wraps up the HERE COME THE BRIDES series with the heartwarming story of a hometown hero who convinces his childhood sweetheart to become his *Expectant Bride-To-Be*.

I hope all of these breathtaking romances warm your hearts and add joy to your holiday season.

Best,
Karen Taylor Richman
Senior Editor

Please address questions and book requests to:
Silhouette Reader Service
U.S.: 3010 Walden Ave., P.O. Box 1325, Buffalo, NY 14269
Canadian: P.O. Box 609, Fort Erie, Ont. L2A 5X3

Expectant Bride-To-Be

NIKKI BENJAMIN

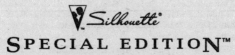

Silhouette®

SPECIAL EDITION™

Published by Silhouette Books

America's Publisher of Contemporary Romance

Special thanks and acknowledgment are given
to Nikki Benjamin for her contribution
to the Here Come the Brides series.

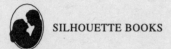

SILHOUETTE BOOKS

ISBN 0-373-24368-5

EXPECTANT BRIDE-TO-BE

Copyright © 2000 by Harlequin Books S.A.

Visit Silhouette at www.eHarlequin.com

Printed in U.S.A.

Books by Nikki Benjamin

NIKKI BENJAMIN

was born and raised in the Midwest, but after years in the Houston area, she considers herself a true Texan. Nikki says she's always been an avid reader. (Her earliest literary heroines were Nancy Drew, Trixie Belden and Beany Malone.) Her writing experience was limited, however, until a friend started penning a novel and encouraged Nikki to do the same. One scene led to another, and soon she was hooked.

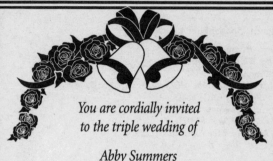

You are cordially invited
to the triple wedding of

Abby Summers
&
Jack Randall

AND

Jessica Walker
&
Sam Dawson

AND

Sarah Daniels
&
Ryan Noble

Reception hosted by Stuart Walker,
at the Walker mansion,
Willow Springs, Nevada

Chapter One

A chill breeze swept across the town square of Promise, Nevada, adding to the dank, dreary feeling of the gray, late-December day. With the onset of early evening, only a few people still bustled down the sidewalks, most more than likely heading for home since the stores would be closing soon.

She should go home, too, Abby Summers thought. Or rather, she should go back to her mother's house. But she continued to sit on the narrow wooden bench facing the small park in the square's center, her hands stuffed deep in the pockets of her black wool coat, her chin tipped down to take advantage of the upturned collar, and her stocking-clad legs tucked together under the full skirt of her calf-length, black wool dress. There were too many memories waiting for her at Larissa's house—memories tinged with sadness.

How Abby wished she had made an effort to know her mother better. With the optimism of youth, she had always assumed that one day they would find the time to sit down and talk like friends. Not so much about the past. That would have been nice. But nicer still, to Abby's way of thinking, maybe they could have shared their hopes and dreams for the future.

Now it was too late.

Abby had returned to the slow, steady farming community two hundred miles northeast of Las Vegas for the Christmas holiday, hoping that she and Larissa might finally embark on a closer relationship. She had even taken a few carefully hoarded days of vacation from her job as a certified public accountant with a firm in San Francisco so this particular visit wouldn't be quite as rushed as the visits she had made in the past. Her grandparents, Hank and Judith, had been delighted, and Larissa herself had seemed pleased.

Abby had arrived at her mother's house on Christmas Eve to find all three waiting for her. Listening to Christmas carols playing on the radio, they trimmed the tree Hank had bought that morning, then tucked into the sandwiches and chocolate chip cookies Judith had provided before making an early night of it.

Larissa's joy in spending the holiday with her family seemed to carry over into Christmas Day. She and Abby went to Hank and Judith's tiny apartment in the senior citizens' complex where they'd moved the previous year. They had opened gifts, then feasted on roast turkey with all the trimmings. By late afternoon, however, Abby had begun to sense her mother's growing discontent—the same discontent that had sent her looking for greener pastures since Abby had been a child.

Leaving her daughter with Hank and Judith, just as she'd done so many times in the past, Larissa had taken off yet again. There was a friend waiting for her in Vegas; a friend who had a friend who just might be able to give her a little work in his casino after the first of the year. Not as a dancer—at least not right away. But once she got on the payroll, waiting tables, surely she'd have a chance to move up the ladder.

That was the last Abby and her grandparents had seen of Larissa until the call that woke Abby just before midnight on December 26. A kindly police officer had advised her that her mother had been killed in a car accident. The man who had been driving, a stranger to Abby, had been drunk. He'd run off the road and hit a tree, and though he had walked away virtually unharmed, Larissa had died at the scene.

Abby had waited until morning to tell her grandparents the devastating news. Then, she'd set about making arrangements for her mother's funeral, refusing to acknowledge her own grief in order to be strong for Hank and Judith.

Considering Larissa's reputation around town as a ne'er-do-well, the number of people at the service that afternoon had been a tribute to her grandparents. For their sake, Abby had been grateful.

Hank and Judith had wanted to linger at the cemetery following the committal, but Abby had insisted on taking them home. Both had been too exhausted to remain outdoors longer than absolutely necessary, especially on such a bleak day, when the chill breeze held in it a threat of rain. Abby hadn't wanted either one of them to risk getting sick. They were the only family she'd ever really had, and she loved them more than anything.

Promising to stop by the next morning before she headed back to San Francisco, Abby had left them in their snug little apartment, sipping mugs of freshly brewed tea. She had gone back to her mother's house to finish packing, but after parking her rental car in the driveway, she had decided to go for a walk instead. Just to gather her thoughts, she'd told herself as she set out. She'd ended up in the town square almost an hour later, and there she'd stayed, alone with her regrets.

Larissa had loved her in her own way. Of that, Abby had always been sure. And she must have wanted her. Otherwise, why would she have brought her into the world? Surely it would have been easier for her to have an abortion than to take on the role of unwed mother, even as erratically as she'd played the part, between the jobs and the men who had kept her, often literally, in Las Vegas.

A short gust of wind caught a wisp of Abby's shoulder-length, auburn hair, tugging it free of the sensible braid she'd woven that morning. The scent of rain filled the air and the sky seemed much darker than it had only a few minutes ago. Time to go, she decided. The walk back to her mother's house would take at least thirty minutes, and she didn't want to get caught in a downpour. She couldn't afford to get sick either. Not with April 15 only a few months away, and her firm's busiest time of year just ahead.

Sliding the strap of her purse over her shoulder, Abby stood slowly. Another gust of wind whipped around her legs, teasing at the hem of her coat and making her shiver. She wished she hadn't dallied quite so long. Now a brisk pace alone wouldn't be enough to chase the chill from her bones.

What she wanted, *needed,* was a cup of coffee, and she knew just where she could get one. From across the square, a brightly lit café beckoned. New to town since her last visit, it looked inviting, and it wasn't too far out of her way.

Aware that she was postponing the inevitable return to her mother's house yet again, Abby set off across the little park. She had gone only a few steps when she caught sight of a man sitting on one of the benches along the gravel path. He was dressed all in black—tailored slacks, turtleneck sweater and leather bomber jacket—and his blond head was bent, his face turned slightly, his expression unusually grim.

Though he seemed as oblivious to her presence as she'd been to his, Abby hesitated, a frown creasing her forehead. While his posture didn't appear the least bit menacing, there was something about him that gave her pause. Then, with a shock of recognition, she draw a sharp breath.

Jack Randall, she thought, her heart fluttering in a truly maddening way.

The star quarterback of the high school football team and son of the wealthy Randall family, Jack had grown up the golden boy of Promise, Nevada. He had also been Abby's champion when she was a lowly freshman and he a lordly senior. He had taken her under his wing when he'd seen her being teased by a group of mean-spirited girls, and he had made a point of looking out for her in a brotherly way for the remainder of the school year. And quite foolishly,

Abby had fallen in love with him even though he'd already had a very special girlfriend to whom he'd been devoted.

Jack had married Cindy Willis as Abby had known he would. They moved to Boston where they both attended college. A few years later, Abby had left Promise as well, going to Stanford on an academic scholarship. But each time she'd returned to Promise, she'd thought about Jack and hoped he was happy. Then, on one of her visits home, she'd heard that Cindy had been killed in a car accident just after Jack's graduation from medical school.

He must have returned to Promise for the holidays just as she had, and he must still be on his own. Otherwise, he wouldn't be sitting in the park, looking as lonely as she'd been feeling.

For one very long, very indecisive moment, Abby was tempted to go up to him and say hello. He had been her friend, after all, and she owed him more than she could ever repay for all the kindness he'd shown her.

But that had been years ago. He probably wouldn't recognize her now, and even if he did, she doubted he'd welcome her intrusion. Jack Randall could have had all the company he wanted, but, for whatever reason, he'd chosen to be alone. She didn't feel right about foisting herself upon him just for old times' sake.

Ducking her head to shield her face, Abby continued down the path. She walked briskly, eyes straight ahead, and hoped that the crunch of her low-heeled shoes on the gravel wouldn't attract his attention. As she passed the bench, she saw him glance her way, but she didn't allow her strides to falter as she headed for the café.

Chapter Two

Jack Randall had seen the auburn-haired woman sitting on a bench across the way when he'd first entered the park in Promise's town square, but he hadn't paid much attention to her. She had been sitting with her head bent so he hadn't been able to see her face, and he'd been too busy feeling sorry for himself to spare her more than a cursory glance.

Home for the Christmas holiday, Jack had found himself missing Cindy more than ever despite the four years that had passed since her death. They had known each other for what seemed like forever. Their parents had been good friends, and since he and Cindy had both been only children, their camaraderie had come naturally. Each of them had filled a void in the other's life as no one else seemed able to do. For years, they had been best buddies, and then, during high school, their relationship had become much more intimate.

Their parents hadn't wanted them to marry the summer after their high school graduation, but he and Cindy had been too much in love to be deterred. They might have been young, but they had known what they wanted. And, against all odds, their love had survived the rigors of their undergraduate years as well as the long hours Jack put in during medical school.

They had made plans—so many plans—for the years they'd assumed they would have ahead of them. With his graduation from medical school and his internship at Texas Children's Hospital in Houston about to begin, their future together had held all the promise they could ever have hoped for. Cindy would be able to give up her job teaching kindergarten, and they would finally be able to start the family they wanted more than anything.

Then a drunk driver had rammed his pickup truck into Cindy's little sports car.

For a long time after her death, the only thing that had kept Jack going was the certainty that she wouldn't have wanted him to curl up and die on her behalf. Somehow he'd managed to pull himself together. He had devoted himself to his work, making the most of his ability to help other people's children overcome the effects of serious illness. He'd had no time for emotional entanglements, but he hadn't really cared. He had loved once, and lost. For him, once was enough.

The unexpected sound of footsteps crunching along the gravel path drew Jack from his reverie. Glancing sideways, he saw the auburn-haired woman was now walking toward him. Despite the waning light, there was something familiar about her face. For several moments, he eyed her surreptitiously, trying to recall where he'd seen her before.

Quite suddenly, it came to him, along with a rush of emotion that left him feeling oddly confused. Abby Summers, he thought, then looked away as she drew closer.

She had been such a sweet, shy girl all those years ago. She hadn't deserved the cruel teasing about her mother's less-than-stellar reputation that she'd been forced to endure her first few weeks at Promise High School. He and Cindy had been appalled by the behavior of their fellow students. Together, they had decided that by befriending her, they could shield her with their own popularity.

Initially, Jack had meant only to be kind to Abby as an act of charity. But very soon, he had realized she was a young lady well worth knowing. She had been a bit gawky, then, and she'd dressed in plain, oversized clothes that hid what shape she had. She'd also worn glasses that had given her an owlish look, and she'd kept her luscious auburn hair pulled back in a braid. But she'd been smart, and as she'd opened up to him, he had found that she also had a delightful sense of humor. Talking to her had never failed to brighten his day.

By the end of his senior year, her freshman year, she had gained the necessary poise and confidence she'd lacked in September. He had known she would be able to get by on her own in the future, and when he heard that she'd left Promise to attend Stanford on a full scholarship, he had been happy for her.

Trying not to appear obvious, Jack followed

Abby's progress along the pathway from the corner of his eye. A few feet from him, she raised her head slightly, giving him an even better look at her lovely face. His little Abby had grown into an elegant young woman—tall and slender, yet nicely rounded in all the right places.

For one long moment, Jack was tempted to stand and greet her, but then, he hesitated. If Abby remembered him at all, it would likely be in the vaguest possible way—a way she might not care to acknowledge.

They had been friends for only nine months, and that had been more than a decade ago. She had evidently changed quite a bit since then—the contact lenses that had obviously replaced her glasses and stylish way she was dressed assured him of that. She might not appreciate being reminded of the past she'd worked so hard to leave behind.

In a quandary, Jack kept his eyes averted as Abby walked past him, though he hoped, perversely, that *she* would glance *his* way, and say something. She moved along briskly, however, her long strides exuding grace and confidence, her eyes on the ground, her hands shoved in her coat pockets.

He should let her go. Really, he should. They had gone their separate ways a long time ago, and that had been for the best. Any encounter he initiated now would be of the briefest duration. And he would probably stir up more discomfort for Abby, as well as himself, than it would be worth.

But how nice it would be to talk to someone who had known him when he'd been young, carefree and happy. He hadn't been that person since Cindy's death. Now, sitting on a lonely park bench with twi-

light falling around him, he wanted to be his old self
again, as he could in the eyes of a former friend like
Abby Summers.

Giving himself no time for second thoughts, Jack
stood quickly and headed after Abby. He caught up
to her as she came to the sidewalk that ran alongside
one of the square's four main streets, reached out and
touched the sleeve of her coat at the same moment
he spoke her name.

"Abby? Abby Summers, right? It's me,
Jack...Jack Randall."

She halted immediately, but seemed to hesitate before she finally turned to face him. Though she
smiled slightly as she met his gaze, her reluctance
was obvious. He wondered if she had recognized him
earlier, but chose, for whatever reason, not to let him
know it.

"Hello, Jack," she said at last, a catch in her
husky voice.

Noting the wariness in her eyes, Jack suffered a
pang of remorse. She had come to the park on her
own because she'd wanted to spend some time alone,
and here he was, not only encroaching upon the pri-
vacy she'd sought, but expecting her to be glad of it,
too.

So say something, *anything*, you idiot, he chas-
tised himself. Finish what you've started and let her
be on her way.

"I see you're home for the Christmas holiday,
too," he said, trying for a lighthearted tone to match
his smile. "Having a nice time, so far?"

She stared at him for several seconds, then looked
away, a frown creasing her forehead.

"Actually, not as nice as I'd hoped," she replied.

"My…my mother died earlier in the week. Her funeral was today."

Recalling an article he'd read in the paper a couple of days ago about a local woman, Larissa Summers, who'd been killed in a car accident, Jack realized why the woman's name had sounded familiar to him. She had been Abby's mother, the one whose antics had brought him and Abby together, in a roundabout way, twelve years ago.

"I'm so sorry for your loss," he began, then added awkwardly, "I didn't know…."

Actually, he should have, and he *would* have if he'd taken the time to put two and two together. But he couldn't tell Abby that. He'd been insensitive enough already.

"Thank you." Brushing away the single tear that trickled down her cheek, she glanced at him. "It was so unexpected. I'm having a hard time accepting that she's really gone."

Abby looked so forlorn that Jack wanted to put his arms around her and hold her close. But his certainty that such a move on his part would be wholly inappropriate, not to mention totally unwelcome, kept him from doing it.

"I understand how you feel," he said instead.

"Yes, you would, wouldn't you?" She met his gaze again, her sympathy and understanding evident. "I can only imagine how devastating Cindy's death was for you."

"She was a very special person. One of a kind, in fact. Going on without her hasn't been easy, but I know that's what she would have wanted me to do. I've been lucky to have my work in pediatric medicine to keep me busy. That's helped a lot."

"You couldn't have chosen a better way to honor her memory," Abby assured him. "She'd be so proud of you."

"I hope so."

Oddly disquieted by the warmth of Abby's gaze, Jack looked away. Once again, the urge to hold her close rode through him, this time as a means to gain comfort as much as to give it. Once again, he refused to allow himself to act upon it.

"Well, I should be going," Abby said after a few moments, shivering delicately as a gust of wind swirled around them.

Common sense dictated that he offer a final word of condolence, wish her well, and wave her on her way, but Jack didn't like that idea at all. Not when he'd felt more at ease with Abby during the few minutes they'd spent together than he'd felt with anyone since Cindy's death. But neither did he want to linger at the edge of the park, trying to make small talk.

So think of an alternative, smart guy.

"Anywhere special?" he asked, trying to buy a little time as his gaze settled on the brightly lit café across the street and an idea began to take shape.

"My mother's house. I've got a few things to do before I fly back to San Francisco tomorrow afternoon."

Ah, San Francisco… He wanted to hear about how she'd ended up there, among other things.

"Have you made any plans for dinner?"

"Not really," she admitted, seeming slightly bemused by his questioning.

"Me, neither. Maybe we could grab a bite to eat

together, for old times' sake," he suggested. "That place across the street looks inviting."

"Oh, I don't know...." she demurred, wary of him once again.

"I know you've probably got a lot to do, but we shouldn't have to wait for a table this early in the evening," he said, then added hurriedly, hoping to reassure her, "I won't keep you long. In fact, I promise I'll have you home by seven at the latest."

For several agonizing moments, Abby stood silently, looking down at the sidewalk. Then, just when Jack was sure she was going to refuse his invitation, she met his gaze and smiled wryly.

"All right," she agreed. "For old times' sake."

Jack couldn't remember the last time he'd been so pleased by the prospect of buying a woman dinner. He had tried it a few times during the past year, just to keep his matchmaking friends happy, but he hadn't had a very good time. Tonight would be different, though. Tonight he'd be with a good friend— a friend who knew and understood him.

They could spend a couple of hours enjoying each other's company, then go their separate ways, the better for having been together. At least, he was sure he would be better for it.

And he would do his best to make sure Abby was, too, he vowed, taking her by the arm as they started across the street. Considering how little choice he'd given her in the matter, that was the least he could do...the very least.

Chapter Three

Abby walked with Jack to the street corner, then stood beside him quietly, waiting for the light to change so they could cross to the other side.

She willed herself to say something that wouldn't sound silly, but thoughts of what she was about to do made it impossible for her to be clever. And the pressure of Jack's hand on her upper arm, though barely perceptible through the heavy fabric of her coat, was making her heart flutter in a most distracting way.

Abby couldn't believe she'd had the temerity to accept Jack's dinner invitation. In fact, she couldn't believe he'd asked her in the first place, even for old times' sake. Yet, he had, and she had, and now here she was, making herself a nervous wreck over what would certainly prove to be nothing more than another of his many acts of kindness.

He hadn't asked her out on a *date,* after all. Just an early dinner at a nearby café for a couple of old friends who had nothing better to do—with the re-assuringly meant promise to have her home by seven tacked on for good measure.

Hearing about her mother's death, he'd probably felt sorry for her, and as he had all those years ago when he'd bought her a soft drink in the high school cafeteria, he'd simply wanted to cheer her up. With his unerring knack for doing the right thing at the right time, he'd decided that taking her to dinner would be the most likely way to revive her sagging spirits.

And he'd been right, Abby conceded as they stepped off the curb. Though her sadness at losing Larissa in such an untimely manner would never dis-appear completely, she no longer felt quite as weighed down by it as she had earlier. For that alone, she owed Jack Randall…yet again.

She wouldn't make more of his invitation than he'd intended, though. Having dinner with Jack at a fine restaurant, preferably by candlelight, had been one of her many youthful fantasies, but she was older now, and wise enough to know that the reality wasn't going to be romantic in the least. They would spend a little time together in a brightly lit neighborhood café, and that would be that.

"Well, here we are," Jack said, stating the obvi-ous as they walked up to the café's old-fashioned, wood-and-glass front door.

Her reverie duly interrupted, Abby looked up at him and smiled. "Yes, here we are," she agreed. Then, aware that, up close, the place looked vaguely familiar, she asked, "Wasn't this a country store years ago?"

"You're right. It was a country store for years. I remember my mother mentioning something about a young couple buying one of the old buildings along the square about a year ago and turning it into a restaurant. This must be the place. She also said the food was supposed to be good. I, for one, hope she's right because I'm famished."

"How are your parents?" Abby glanced up at Jack as he opened the door for her, suddenly curious about why he wasn't having dinner with *them.*

He had already said he'd come home for the holidays. Surely the Randalls would have wanted to show off their handsome, successful son every chance they had. Jack had been quite popular in his own right, as well, and many of his old friends either lived in Promise or had family there, themselves. It struck her as odd that he was so obviously at loose ends during what she'd always considered the height of the small town's social season.

"They're doing fine," Jack replied. "My father retired from the bank almost a year ago. Since then, he and my mother have been traveling a lot. They left this afternoon to celebrate New Year's on a Caribbean cruise. They'll be gone a couple of weeks. I couldn't take the time off to join them, and I couldn't get a flight back to Houston until tomorrow morning, so..." He shrugged, offering her a slight smile as they entered the café.

"Too bad," Abby said, though she didn't really mean it. Selfish as it might be, she was glad Jack had been stuck in Promise an extra day. "Celebrating

New Year's on a Caribbean cruise sounds wonderful.''

"It would have been if I'd had someone special to share it with."

The way Jack held her gaze for an extra beat as they stood in the doorway, halfway between the dark chill of twilight and the café's mellow, glowing warmth, had Abby thinking he didn't mean Cindy. But only until she gave herself a firm mental shake. Walking ahead of him, she ordered herself to stop the foolish fantasizing, then smiled at the young woman who stepped forward to greet them.

"Two for dinner?" she asked, welcoming them with a smile of her own.

"Yes, please," Jack answered.

"I can take your coats if you'd like?"

"Okay with you?" he asked, touching Abby lightly on the shoulder.

She nodded agreeably, unbuttoning her coat as she looked around the cafe. Though the place was larger than it appeared from the outside, there was a cozy, country-home feel to it. The furnishings had an antique look complemented by the lace curtains on the windows. Despite the early hour, two couples and a family of four had already been seated, and as Jack helped her out of her coat, the door opened and another family entered.

"Looks like we got here just in time," she said.

"Yeah, another thirty minutes and we probably would have had to wait. Then I'd never have been able to get you home by seven, and I'd have been in big trouble."

Though Jack spoke the words in a serious tone,

the mischievous twinkle in his eyes warned Abby that he really didn't consider *big trouble* a bad thing.

"How about a table by the fireplace?" the hostess suggested after she'd hung up their coats.

"Sound good to you?" Once again, Jack deferred to Abby, making her feel special in a subtle, but important, way.

"Sounds great," she replied. "Why don't you go on ahead and I'll join you after I call my grandparents. I want to let them know where I am in case they need me for any reason. I promise I'll only be a few minutes."

"No problem. Take your time." He gave her arm a heartening squeeze. "Would you like me to order a drink for you—a glass of wine, or something stronger?"

"A glass of red wine would be lovely," she said, shooting him a wry smile.

"Ah, a woman after my own heart." He smiled, too, then turned to follow the hostess as she led the way to their table.

Abby made a quick stop in the rest room to pull herself together. There wasn't much she could do about her puffy eyes, but at least her hair had stayed neatly in place, and a dab of fresh lipstick brightened her pale face. Reminding herself yet again that she wasn't on a date, and she looked just fine for a spur-of-the-moment dinner with a friend, she then called her grandparents on the pay phone she found in the narrow hallway that led back to the dining room.

Her grandmother answered after several rings, her voice sounding weary. Afraid that she'd awakened her from a much-needed nap, Abby told her about meeting Jack in the park and her acceptance of his dinner invitation.

Judith's tone cheered immediately.

"Jack Randall? He's that nice young man who was so kind to you when you were in high school, isn't he?" she asked.

"Yes, that's him."

"Well, you enjoy your evening out, Abby. You certainly deserve it. Don't worry about your grandfather and me. We'll be just fine."

"Are you sure, Gran?"

"I'm sure, sweetie."

"I'll see you in the morning then. Before I leave for the airport."

"Come for breakfast and bring your young man," Judith said.

"Oh, Gran, he's not my young man. But I will come for breakfast…on my own."

Leave it to her grandmother to make something out of nothing. She meant well, of course. She wanted Abby to settle down with a good man and have babies. Abby wouldn't have minded that herself, but she hadn't met the right man yet. And Jack wasn't the one, either—no matter how she wished he could be. There were all sorts of obstacles in the way. They didn't even live in the same city, and that was just for starters.

Warning herself not to spoil what time they did have together with maudlin thoughts, Abby finally joined Jack at their table by the fireplace. He stood as she walked toward him and held her chair with gentlemanly care. When they were both seated, he poured a glass of wine for her from the bottle on the table.

"To old friends," he said, raising his glass to her. "And fond memories."

"Yes." She smiled as she clinked her glass to his. "To old friends and fond memories."

As she sipped from her glass, Abby admired the way the firelight burnished Jack's golden-blond hair. He had been a very handsome young man all those years ago. Maturity had only added to his masculine appeal. But his appearance alone wasn't what attracted Abby the most.

He had a way of looking at her that made her feel like the most important person in the world. When he spoke, it was never with condescension, and when he offered help, he never thought of what might be in it for him. He had never used his wealth or social standing in town to lord it over others who were less fortunate. Instead, he had sought out ways to make a difference, as he had in her life, and he continued to do the same in his chosen profession.

"You're looking rather pensive," Jack said, eyeing her curiously as he set his wine glass aside. "What are you thinking?"

"That I'm glad I agreed to have dinner with you," Abby admitted, unable to be anything but honest with him.

There was no reason why she couldn't take pleasure in his company for whatever time they had together, and no reason why she had to keep her pleasure a secret.

"Not half as glad as I am." He flashed a rueful grin as he handed her one of the menus their waitress had left on the table. "You've saved me from a night of rattling around my parents' house, all alone. If we weren't here together, I'd be sitting in front of the television set, eating yet another in a long line of turkey sandwiches.''

When Jack shuddered for emphasis, Abby couldn't help but laugh.

''I can't tell you how pleased I am to have spared you *that* awful fate.''

''Why don't you try?'' he suggested, a mischievous look in his eyes.

''Jack, oh, Jack, I'm *so* happy you're not sitting all alone in front of the television set, eating yet another in a long line of turkey sandwiches,'' she gushed, then blushed as she realized how silly she must sound.

Her embarrassment lasted only an instant, though. Leaning across the table, Jack took her hand in his and replied with equal fervency, ''Abby, oh, Abby, I'm so happy, too.''

They laughed together, then Jack lifted his glass in another toast that Abby seconded, to anything but yet another turkey sandwich. Finally, they opened their menus.

They both ordered the special of the day, beef Stroganoff, along with Caesar salad. Then Jack asked Abby about her life in San Francisco. His interest was so sincere that she had no trouble telling him about her job at one of the city's top-tier accounting firms and the delightful little town house she'd bought recently just a cable-car ride from the office.

As they dug into their salads, he asked, too, if she was seeing anyone special, and Abby said, quite truthfully, that she wasn't.

In fact, there had been two men in her life since she'd left Promise—a dark-haired, broody, James Dean type she'd dated while she was at Stanford, and the CFO of a small engineering company she'd met at a conference. He had been nice enough, but during their year-long relationship, which had ended almost six months ago, Abby had come to think of him as Mr. Beige, in deference to his personality as well as the clothes he often chose to wear.

Of course, she didn't tell Jack any of that. Instead, she turned the conversation to *his* life in Houston.

By the time they'd finished their main course and chosen a dessert to share with their coffee—a slice of decadently rich chocolate cheesecake in a pecan crust—Abby realized that Jack had been serious when he'd said he had devoted himself to his work since Cindy's death. He socialized even less than she did, and then only at functions sponsored by the hospital where he was completing his residency in pediatric medicine.

"How much longer will you be at Texas Children's Hospital?" Abby asked as she helped herself to a forkful of cheesecake.

"About two months. My residency will be over at the end of February."

"Then what will you do?"

"I'm trying to decide," Jack replied, frowning thoughtfully. "I've had several offers to join established medical practices, including one here in Promise. An internist and an obstetrician teamed up to open a clinic about a year ago, and they're looking for a pediatrician to sign on so they'll be able to offer even more comprehensive care to their patients."

"Would you like to come back here to live and work?"

Personally, she couldn't think of anything she would rather do *less*. Of course, Jack had had a much easier time of it growing up in Promise. He'd truly been a favored son, in more ways than one.

"I'm not sure. I've been gone a long time, and I've gotten used to living in big cities. But I could really make a difference at the clinic here. More than I could in the other practices I've been considering." He met her gaze and smiled. "How about you? Have you ever thought about living in Promise again?"

"Not at all," she stated succinctly. Then, aware that her voice had sounded harsher than she'd intended, she smiled as she added, "I'm more than happy where I am, thank you very much."

"More bad memories than good for you here?" he asked, his concern for her evident.

"In some respects." Abby shrugged noncommittally as their waitress paused by their table to serve more coffee.

"Are you ready for your check, sir?" she asked after refilling their cups.

"Yes, please," Jack replied, then glanced at his watch as she walked away. "Oh, no. I'm about to be in big trouble."

"Why is that?" Abby asked, smiling at his suddenly sheepish expression.

"I promised I'd have you home by seven and it's now almost eight o'clock."

"You're kidding."

Abby couldn't believe so much time had passed. It seemed as if they'd only just arrived minutes, not hours, ago.

"I'm sorry, Abby. I really lost track of time."

"Don't apologize, Jack. So did I."

"I haven't had such an enjoyable evening out in…years."

"Neither have I. Thanks for making this such a lovely dinner."

"My pleasure."

He held her gaze for several long moments, his expression so warm, so sincere, that Abby wished their time together was only just beginning rather than ending as it most surely must.

When the waitress arrived with their bill, Jack finally looked away. Pulling out his wallet, he overrode her initial protest that they split the bill, and paid for their meal. The hostess had their coats ready for them by the time they reached the entryway, and a few minutes later they were standing on the sidewalk.

As they paused to adjust their collars against the chill wind, the fine mist of rain that had begun to fall left tiny droplets of moisture sparkling on their hair. Looking around, Abby saw that the shops surrounding the square had turned on their Christmas lights. Several of the tress in the park were lit up, as well, giving the place a magical glow. Or maybe it was standing there with Jack Randall that made Promise, Nevada suddenly seem so enchanting.

"Well, thanks again," she said at last, her good, old-fashioned pragmatism coming to the fore as she held out her hand. "I really enjoyed seeing you."

It was getting late, and she had a long walk back to her mother's house ahead of her, not to mention a Christmas tree to take down, decorations to put away and her suitcase to pack. She didn't have time to linger, especially when it would do her more harm than good. The sooner she parted company with Jack, the sooner she would stop fantasizing about impossible, improbable what-ifs.

"I'd feel better if you let me walk you to your car. I realize you're probably parked close by, but I'd just...feel better." He took her hand, holding on to it far longer than necessary.

"Actually, I walked here from my mother's house," Abby admitted. "And I don't mind walking back on my own. After the meal we just had, the exercise will do me good, and Promise is pretty quiet this time of night. I don't think I'll run into trouble between here and there."

"Well, I'm not about to let you take any chances." He tucked her hand in the crook of his arm and drew her into step beside him as he started down the sidewalk. "My rental car is parked on the other side of the square. Come along, and I'll give you a ride home."

"Do I have a choice?" she asked, lifting an eyebrow as she glanced at him.

"None at all," he answered with a wicked grin.

"All right, then." Looking away, Abby smiled, too.

She could have found a way to refuse his offer—she probably *should* have. But he only had her best interests at heart. And, quite frankly, she *liked* walking down the street arm-in-arm with Jack Randall. The way he moved along, close beside her, made her feel...treasured. Walking to her mother's house alone on a night like tonight would have been downright miserable in comparison.

They made the short drive in relative silence. Abby gave directions and Jack followed them, driving at a moderate speed in deference to the weather and the dark, narrow streets.

"I can't believe you considered walking all this

way alone,'' he said when they had only gone about half the distance, the merest hint of anger in his voice.

''It wouldn't have been the first time,'' she replied quite honestly, causing him to mutter something unintelligible under his breath.

Abby wanted to remind him that not everyone had had parents to drive them wherever they wanted to go, not to mention wheels of their own from the age of sixteen on, but she didn't want to spoil what little time they had left with a lecture.

At the house, Jack pulled into the driveway behind her rental car, then caught hold of her arm as she started to unfasten her seat belt.

''Don't even think about getting out of the car until I come around and open the door for you,'' he said.

''Believe it or not, I've gotten out of cars on my own quite a few times, too.'' She glanced at him with a slight smile. ''I've even walked up to the front porch and let myself into the house alone without any problems.''

''I'm sure you have. Tonight you're with me, though. And it's my duty, as a gentleman, to see you to your front door. As your old friend, Jack Randall, it's also something I'd like very much to do.''

''In that case, I promise not to budge until you say so.''

As good as his word, Jack helped Abby out of the car and walked with her to the front porch, one hand resting gently at the small of her back. Then he waited patiently as she fit her key into the lock and opened the door.

As she turned to say goodbye to him, Abby was

glad she'd remembered to leave the outside light on. At least she had the chance to get one last look at his handsome face before they finally parted—a look she would remember always.

"Well, thanks...yet again," she said, smiling despite the sudden ache in her heart. She could be as reasonable as she wanted about the snowball's chance in hell she had of ever running into Jack Randall again, but that didn't make it any easier to accept. "Tonight was just...wonderful."

"I thought so, too." He gazed at her searchingly, then looked away as he shoved his hands in the pockets of his black leather jacket. "I'm sorry to see it end."

"Not half as sorry as I am," Abby admitted, parroting a comment he'd made earlier in the evening, her tone only half-teasing.

"You know, we don't have to say good-night just yet." He faced her again, his green eyes glinting hopefully. "You could offer me a drink. I'd accept."

Abby couldn't think of anything she'd rather do, but prolonging the agony of their eventual parting was getting harder and harder for her. She had braced herself for the moment several times already, hiding her true feelings behind a mask of casual nonchalance.

Too much longer in his presence, and she just might throw herself at his feet—

"I know you have a lot to do," Jack added, seeming to sense her hesitation. "So if you'd prefer not to, I'll understand."

"Actually, I'd like you to stay," Abby said, tossing common sense to the wind without a second thought.

What was another hour or so in the general scheme of things? Especially when Jack was merely postponing the moment when he'd have to go back to his parents' empty house. She wasn't in any big hurry to be alone herself.

"Really?" he asked, his green eyes gleaming with pleasure.

"Yes, really," she assured him, smiling as she took him by the hand and led him into the house.

Chapter Four

Jack followed Abby into her mother's small, wood-frame bungalow, trying not to feel too embarrassed by his neediness. He had fully intended to see that she got home safely, then be on his way. But by the time they got to the modest neighborhood where she'd grown up, he could hardly bear the thought of spending the rest of the evening alone.

Being with Abby had brightened his spirits enormously. In fact, he couldn't remember enjoying a woman's company so much since he'd been on his own. Odd, because Abby wasn't anything at all like Cindy. She was smart and funny in her own very special way—a way that appealed to him even more than he'd originally anticipated.

Taking Abby out to dinner hadn't turned out to be quite as casual an affair as he'd intended—at least not for him. Her presence across the table had filled him with a warm glow of contentment. Selfishly, perhaps, he'd wanted to hang on to that long-forgotten feeling.

He'd coerced her into offering him a drink before he could think better of it, and he'd been so relieved when she agreed. Just a quick drink, then he'd go. Or so Jack had told himself until the moment she took him by the hand and led him into the house.

The first flicker of an altogether different, not to mention far more intimate, yearning sizzled along his nerve endings, while low down in his belly, another kind of warmth began to uncurl. And no matter how insistently he told himself to ignore it, he was intrigued by the heretofore unthought-of possibility that suddenly came to mind.

He should leave *now*. He should, but hell if he could—

"Is something wrong?" Abby asked, looking up at him with a slight frown. She had stepped into the tiny entryway, still holding his hand, while he stood, as if rooted to the spot, on the threshold.

"No, not at all," Jack assured her, making a valiant effort to pull himself together as he joined her.

"You don't have to stay if you've thought of something you need to do instead," she added, letting go of his hand.

He had, but not in the way she meant. And though she'd given him an easy way out that he should gratefully take, he wasn't going to do it. He had resigned himself to living what had become a very lonely life. He hadn't realized how much he'd missed the feelings now coursing through him—the comfort of companionship laced with the heat of desire, the wanting and needing, ignored for so long, that had reared up when he was least expecting it.

"No, there's nothing." He looped an arm loosely around her shoulders, a first foray into territory he was suddenly, unashamedly desperate to explore.

Abby seemed a bit startled by his gesture, but she didn't pull away.

"Well, then, let me take your jacket."

The entryway of the little house opened directly into the living room. With the flick of the light switch on the wall, Abby lit the lamps on a pair of glass-and-brass end tables framing an old sofa upholstered in a faded rose and green floral print. The multicolored lights on the Christmas tree, standing in the far corner, lit up, as well, adding a poignant warmth to the room. An easy chair and ottoman, covered in a green and beige pin-striped fabric, a brass and glass coffee table and matching étagère filled with an assortment of books, porcelain figurines and framed photographs completed the furnishings.

Though Jack was accustomed to more elegant surroundings, he was immediately drawn by the coziness of the room. Here was a place where two people could sit together, close enough to touch, and talk about anything their hearts desired.

"This is nice," he said, reaching back with his free hand to close the front door.

"Thanks," Abby murmured as she stepped free of his hold.

Before he could offer his assistance, she slipped out of her coat and hung it on the old-fashioned, carved oak coat tree that stood off to one side. Then she turned back to him, a quizzical look on her face.

"What?" he asked, not quite sure what was expected of him.

"Your jacket." She smiled slightly. "Unless you've decided not to stay, after all."

"I'm staying." He returned her smile sheepishly as he shrugged out of his jacket and hung it up himself.

He'd been so caught up by the way she'd moved around the entryway—coming so near to him in the close quarters, yet not quite touching—that he'd been able to think of nothing but pulling her into his arms, pushing her up against the wall, kissing her senseless and...more than likely, scaring her half to death. Cursing silently, he gave himself a firm mental shake.

"I'd planned to take down the tree last night, but I just couldn't seem to make myself do it," Abby explained, a hint of apology in her tone as she led him toward the sofa.

"I could give you a hand with it now," Jack offered, glad to take on any task that would not only allow him added time with Abby, but also keep his hands occupied. "Unless you'd rather tackle it alone."

Abby eyed him consideringly for several moments, then glanced away.

"I hate putting you to work when all you were expecting was a drink, but I'd really appreciate the help. As long as you're sure you don't mind."

"I wouldn't have offered otherwise, and it won't take us long, working together."

"At least let me get you a drink first."

As she headed toward the doorway on the left, Jack saw that it led to the kitchen. He followed after her, pausing in the doorway as she turned on the overhead fluorescent light.

"I know there's a bottle of scotch and a bottle of gin in here," she continued, opening one of the lower cabinet doors. "There's tonic for the gin, too, and some brandy of indeterminate age."

"The brandy sounds good to me."

"Me, too," Abby agreed, taking the squat, brown bottle from the cabinet and setting it on the counter.

She found a couple of small snifters in an upper cabinet, poured a generous measure of the liquor into each of them, then offered one to Jack.

Raising her glass, she sniffed tentatively, and smiled. "Smells okay."

Jack, too, inhaled the heady aroma and smiled. "Very nice." He touched the rim of his glass to hers with a faint clink. "Cheers."

"To you, too."

They each took a sip and agreed that it was actually pretty good. Then they walked back to the living room with Abby leading the way and Jack, brandy bottle in hand, turning off the kitchen light as he followed.

Abby set her glass on the coffee table, crossed to a small closet and took out several cardboard boxes. Jack set his glass and the brandy bottle on the table, as well, then walked over to give her a hand.

"I can manage the boxes," she said. "But can you bring the stepladder over? We'll need it to reach the ornaments at the top of the tree."

While Abby arranged the boxes on the coffee table and opened their flaps, Jack positioned the ladder near the tree.

"Ornaments first?" he asked as he climbed the three steps.

"That would probably be best. Then we can figure out how to unwind the strands of lights."

"Why don't I hand you the ornaments? That way, you can pack them up the way you want."

"Sounds good to me," Abby agreed.

They worked quietly for almost thirty minutes, developing an assembly-line kind of rhythm as Jack passed the various ornaments to Abby, who carefully tucked away the nostalgic mix of Santas, snowmen, brightly colored glass globes, and cookie-dough cutouts of all sizes and shapes. Then Jack eased the tree away from the wall and unwound the strings of lights while Abby coiled them into neat bundles.

"That wasn't bad at all," he said as Abby closed up the last of the boxes.

He was inordinately pleased by all they had accomplished together. Taking down the Christmas tree was a job that usually left him feeling sad, even during the best of times. But sharing the job with Abby had actually lightened his spirits.

A glimpse of her somber expression as she carried one of the boxes back to the closet, however, warned him the same wasn't true for her. Of course, it wouldn't be. Not when she'd just lost her mother.

"Let me put these away for you," he said, picking up the two remaining boxes.

"Thanks." She offered him a slight smile, then sat on the sofa, cradling her brandy glass in her hands as she stared at the bare tree.

Jack figured Abby was probably ready for him to leave, but he had no trouble talking himself into staying just a little while longer. She might think that she'd rather be alone with her memories of happier days, but he understood all too well how depressing that could become. He wasn't about to grab his jacket and go just when his company would do her the most good.

He put away the stepladder, then eyed the tree consideringly, hands on his hips.

"I'm guessing I should take this out to the curb for the next trash pickup," he said.

"That would be great. But you don't have to do it right now." Abby patted the sofa cushion beside her. "Come and finish your brandy first. Otherwise I'll feel even guiltier than I already do for making you work so hard."

"There's no need for you to feel guilty at all," Jack assured her as he sat down. "I was glad to help out."

"It was really nice to have the company." Tucking her legs up under her, Abby shifted on the sofa so that she faced him.

"Nice for me, too." Jack sipped his brandy, enjoying the way it warmed him. Although the glow he suddenly felt deep in his belly could have just as easily been ignited by the sweetness of her smile. "I'd forgotten how much fun a chore can be when you share it with someone special."

Abby's eyes lit with surprise, then suddenly, she seemed embarrassed. Blushing, she looked away, took a swallow of her brandy, then another.

"That's very kind of you, Jack, but—"

"Not kind at all," he cut in, reaching out to touch her cheek. Her smooth, soft skin was wonderfully warm against his fingertips. Gently, he turned her face until she met his gaze again. "Honest...I was just being...honest. You're a very special person, Abby Summers. To me, you always have been.''

''You've always been special to me, too,'' she murmured.

Acting purely on instinct—an instinct, old as time, that was deeply rooted in every human being's soul—Jack eased his hand into Abby's hair. Leaning closer to her, he tilted her face up, bent his head and feathered the lightest of kisses across her lips.

Startled, she drew in a sharp breath and started to say something. Before she could speak reason, Jack quickly silenced her, taking her mouth in a deeper, more possessive way that fed the growing hunger pulsing through his loins.

With a barely audible moan, Abby melted against him, her hands clutching the fabric of his turtleneck sweater as she gave herself up to his not-so-tender ministrations. Urged on by the intensity of her response, Jack skimmed his hands over her shoulders, then down to her breasts. Through the layers of her clothing, her nipples pressed hard against his palms, making *him* hard, as well. So hard he could barely keep from crying out at the almost painful pleasure of it.

As Abby's hand drifted down to the buckle of his belt, then lower still, Jack wanted to make himself stop her—stop *them*. He tried to tell himself that he hadn't invited himself into her house because he hoped to have sex with her, but he knew better.

He had been aching for just this kind of release longer than he could remember. And Abby, too, seemed to want, to need, the same affirmation of life their mating would provide. So, instead of pushing her hands away, he offered himself to her with a subtle thrust of his hips.

But you hardly know her, and she's so vulnerable now, his conscience warned.

For one long moment, Jack hesitated, grasping almost desperately for his normally cool self-control. He couldn't, *shouldn't,* make love to her. She would read more into it than he was capable of offering her or any woman.

Then Abby's fingertips traced the rigid length of his erection, and he gave up the battle. He had to have her—had to have her *now* or he would go mad.

With a low groan, he took her hands in his, then broke off their kiss. Immediately, she stiffened and started to pull away.

"Abby, please," he muttered, trailing tiny kisses along her jaw as he put his arms around her. "I want to make love to you, but not on the living room sofa. I want to take you to bed—if you'll let me—so I can do it properly."

She clung to him wordlessly for what seemed like an eternity, then nodded her head. She drew away from him, stood and held out her hand.

Silently, Jack stood, too, took her hand and walked with her to the dark narrow hallway that led to the back of the house.

One last time, his conscience reared up, demanding that he stop before he made a terrible mistake. Then he was standing with Abby in a tiny room, next to a quilt-covered bed that looked barely big enough for the two of them, and suddenly he was reaching out for her, dragging her hard against him and kissing her with a desperation that seemed to know no bounds.

Chapter Five

For Abby, all the years of longing for what she'd so firmly believed she would never have rose up inside her as a mighty tide, and swept away all her inhibitions the moment Jack kissed her. When she had been a freshman in high school, she had accepted that he could never be anything except her friend, but suddenly...

Suddenly, she realized that they could have a deeper, more meaningful relationship now. The kind of relationship that could last a lifetime. Jack was free to love again, and surely he must love her, if only in a new and tentative way, or he wouldn't want to take her to bed.

He had never seemed like the type to use a woman casually to satisfy his sexual needs. And after the hours they had just spent together, talking, she knew he hadn't become that type, either.

Which meant *she* could finally reveal her love for him without fear of being rejected.

As Abby led Jack into her bedroom, she had no second thoughts at all. Jack wanted her with a fierceness so obvious it had taken her breath away. She'd felt it in the pressure of his hands as he'd touched her breasts and her buttocks, and she'd tasted it in the wild, unrelenting passion of his kisses.

Nothing mattered more to her than lying naked with him in her narrow bed. She needed to love and be loved as much as he seemed to. There was no way she could deny herself the glorious moments to come, and no reason that she should.

With his first light-as-rain kiss, Jack had chased away the sense of abandonment that had haunted Abby for as long as she could remember. Tonight she would belong to him, heart and mind, body and soul, as *he* would belong to *her*. And that belonging would empower them both, their love uniting them in a way that would make possible all the things she had never allowed herself to hope for.

Still holding Jack's hand, Abby stopped beside her bed and faced him again. The darkness, broken only by the faint light from the living room outlining the doorway, shadowed his features. But she didn't need to see his face clearly to be reassured of his desire. He didn't hesitate a moment before taking her in his arms again, kissing the side of her neck, then the hollow under her ear, making her shiver with wanton delight.

Seemingly spurred on by her response, he uttered another low groan as he took her mouth in a deep, searing kiss. Rising on the balls of her feet, Abby fit herself to him, undulating against the rigid length of him, eager to feel the proof of his desire as best she could through the layers of clothing they wore.

Jack groaned yet again, his hands moving down her back and tightening on her hips. Then, astonishingly, he broke off their kiss and, breathing hard, took a determined step back. Too startled by his apparent change of heart to speak, Abby gaped at him for a long moment while she fought to catch her own gasping breath.

"I can't protect you," he muttered at last, his voice ragged. "I don't have anything with me. So...unless you do...we have to...stop..."

"Oh, no...I didn't think..." Abby murmured. Totally disoriented, she clutched at the fabric of Jack's sweater as she swayed slightly. She could feel the way his heart raced, much like her own. "And I'm not...I don't—"

She wasn't on the pill and she didn't have any other form of birth control with her. It had been such a long while since she'd been sexually active that she hadn't thought it necessary to carry anything with her. And never, in her wildest dreams, would she have considered the possibility that she'd end up in Promise, Nevada, standing next to her bed, on the verge of making love with Jack Randall.

How she wished she had heeded her mother's long ago advice to *always* keep protection handy—

Moving his hands from her hips to her shoulders, Jack took another step back.

"I'm sorry, Abby. I probably shouldn't have—"

"Wait," she said, her memory of Larissa's advice triggering another recollection.

She had been looking for a fresh box of tissues in the cabinet under the bathroom sink her first night at home, and hidden behind a can of cleanser and several rolls of toilet paper, she'd come across a partially used box of condoms.

Abby had been more amused than anything by her discovery. Her mother had always preached the practice of safe sex. Obviously, she had still been practicing what she preached. And thanks to her diligence, so could she and Jack. As long as Jack was still willing.

"What is it?" he asked, his hands still on her shoulders.

"In the cabinet under the sink in the bathroom...there's a box of condoms. I saw it the other night."

Jack didn't say anything for several seconds, but he didn't release his hold on her, either. Her heart pounding, Abby waited for him to make a decision. Finally, he pulled her close and hugged her, hard.

"I'll get it," he murmured, his voice filled with relief.

"Down the hall to the left," she said as he turned toward the doorway.

Abby waited until he'd left the bedroom, then kicked off her shoes and unzipped her dress. She stepped out of it, set it on the chair by her little desk, then slipped out of her stockings, bra and panties. By the time Jack returned, she had crawled into her bed, scooted over to make room for him, and tucked the quilt up around her shoulders.

Without speaking, Jack set the box of condoms on the nightstand, then turned on the lamp.

Abby's first instinct was to protest. Then, she saw the blaze of desire in Jack's eyes as his gaze roved over her, and she smiled instead.

In response to her unconscious invitation, his jaw seemed to tighten. Still silent, he quickly stripped out of his clothes, then seemed to hesitate again.

Abby stared at him, her mouth going dry as she took in the beauty of his masculinity. When she finally dared to look at his face, she saw that he was now the one smiling, his eyes heavy-lidded, his mouth teasingly seductive.

"So...you approve?" he asked, his voice low.

"Oh, yes. I approve," Abby replied, tossing aside the quilt and patting the empty space beside her.

"Will you do something for me?"

Though Jack slid into bed beside her, he didn't immediately take her in his arms.

"What's that?"

While Abby couldn't think of anything she'd refuse him, the question came out automatically.

"Will you let me take down your hair?" He reached out a tentative hand, curling an already loosened wisp around his finger.

"I most certainly will," she agreed, her smile widening.

Jack made short work of her braid, his fingers deft and clever, yet oh so gentle, as they freed the plait. Then he sifted his hands through the silky strands until he'd spread them over her shoulders in a mass of shimmering waves.

"You are so *damn* beautiful," he muttered, meeting her gaze. "So beautiful..."

He bent his head, growling low in his throat, and kissed her with a hunger that stole her breath away all over again. From one moment to the next, any thought he might have had of holding back seemed to disappear.

As she had earlier, Abby sensed the almost frightening fierceness of his need. Undaunted, she gave herself to him, heart and soul, reveling in the urgent tug of his mouth on her breast and the boldly probing stroke of his fingertips between her legs.

He soon had her writhing and twisting under him, begging with wordless cries and shifting hips for more, and then more again until he covered himself with a condom, and almost in the same movement, plunged so deep inside her she called out his name as her body convulsed.

Rearing back, Jack, too, found release, pounding hard against her as shudder after shudder swept over him.

Afterward, they lay together in a tangle, panting as if they'd run for miles, their bodies hot and damp with sweat. Neither of them spoke, but as Jack held her close, he gently stroked her hair.

Curled against him, her head on his chest, Abby blinked back tears of joy. She had never in her life experienced such an overwhelming sense of fulfillment—the kind of fulfillment that only came with love heartfully given and received.

"I'm sorry I rushed things," Jack said after a while, reaching down to grab the quilt and tuck it up around them. "I really meant to take more time."

"If I remember correctly, you weren't the only one in a hurry," Abby answered, tracing the line of his jaw with her fingertips.

He caught her hand and bit down gently on her wrist, then soothed the spot with a lap of his tongue.

"Still, I should make it up to you," he insisted, meeting her gaze, his eyes mischievous.

"Well, yes, I suppose you should…"

He trailed a line of wet, wanton kisses up the inside of her arm to her shoulder and along the line of her collarbone. Then, using his tongue, he did something truly lascivious to the delicate shell of her ear that had her drawing up her knees in renewed anticipation.

''Well, then, don't go anywhere,'' he murmured as he slipped out of bed.

Abby couldn't have disobeyed him if she'd wanted to. He had turned her bones to jelly, and the sensation was actually quite delightful.

Jack returned within a matter of minutes. One glance at him assured Abby that he intended to waste no time making up for his prior haste. She reached out for him with undisguised eagerness as he snuggled down beside her, but he seemed to have another idea in mind.

Clasping her wrists loosely in one of his hands, Jack stretched her arms over her head. Then he proceeded to show her—very slowly, but very thoroughly—just how shamelessly passionate he could tempt her to be.

Chapter Six

Fighting back yet another wave of panic, Jack forced himself to take slow, deep breaths as he stared into the gradually waning darkness. Beside him in the narrow bed, tucked close to him, spoon-style, Abby slept soundly—one thing, at least, to be grateful for.

Were she to awaken, he would have to talk to her, and in talking to her, he would have to tell her things she wouldn't like hearing.

If only he'd had the sense to quit while he was ahead, Jack thought. Then he wouldn't have put himself in such an untenable position. He'd had so many chances to leave well enough alone since he'd first seen Abby in the park. But he had allowed his baser instincts to get the better of him at each and every turning point.

He could have resisted the urge to kiss her; he

could have stopped short of having sex with her; most important, he could have allowed once to be enough.

Instead, he had gotten himself in deeper than he'd ever intended to be with any woman ever again. And the hell of it was, Abby wasn't just *any* woman. She was someone very special, someone who deserved a better hand than he was about to deal her.

As Jack had followed Abby into her bedroom, he had tried to convince himself that they were two adults capable of having recreational sex without any strings attached. But somewhere in the back of his mind, he had known the intimacies they were about to share would likely hold an altogether different meaning for her.

She had proven him right as he drove into her, at first slow and steady, then harder, faster. The second time he'd taken her, she had clung to him fiercely, meeting him thrust for thrust, crying out as they found release together, then murmuring softly, ''I love you...love you...so much,'' when he cradled her close in his arms.

Oddly enough, her words hadn't upset him then. In fact, in all honesty, hearing them had filled him with pleasure, such pleasure that for a few moments, in the afterglow of their lovemaking, he had thought he loved her, too. He'd even come close to telling her so.

Quickly, though, he had come to his senses.

He'd been in love with Cindy, deeply and completely, and the pain of losing her had been almost more than he could bear. He never wanted to suffer through anything so devastating again. Allowing himself to love Abby—as he had realized he so easily could—would open him up to the possibility of a whole new world of hurt.

Luckily, she had been so exhausted that she'd fallen asleep within a matter of minutes after they'd made love that second time. Gently, he had extricated himself from her arms, gathered his clothes, and slipped down the hall to the bathroom.

Jack had meant to get dressed and leave without waking her. Not exactly the most gentlemanly behavior, but if he stayed, he would very likely say or do something that would only serve to lead Abby on further.

Better to act like the cad he was and free her from any lingering illusions she might harbor than leave her with hopes and dreams he couldn't fulfill.

Then, in the bright light of the bathroom's overhead fixture, Jack had seen something that had him choking back a cry of disbelief. The condom he'd been so careful to use had a very obvious tear in it. The protection against pregnancy he'd meant to offer Abby had been no protection at all.

Stunned, he had cleaned himself up. Instead of dressing, he had gone back to the bedroom and crawled into her bed again. Suddenly, walking out on her without a word had taken on a new and unconscionable twist.

Granted, odds were against his having impregnated her. But there was always a chance, however slight, that the unthinkable could have happened. His child might very well be growing inside her already, and she had a right to know it so that she could take whatever measures she deemed necessary.

Jack didn't like the idea of Abby aborting their child—if such a child actually existed. But he couldn't prevent her from doing it, either. She had a promising career ahead of her, and he seriously doubted that taking on the role of single mother was one of her long-term goals.

What he could do, however, was let her know that if she did choose to take on the responsibility of raising their child, she would be able to count on his financial help. He would provide for her living expenses, hire a full-time nanny for her, pay for the best schools when the time came.

Hell, he would even offer to marry her if the damned rabbit died—

With that thought had come what would be the first of several major panic attacks Jack experienced in the hours he lay awake in Abby's bed.

Marrying Abby was absolutely, positively, out of the question. He simply couldn't do it. Not when he had already come much too close to loving her in the few hours they'd spent together.

She had already said she loved him. If he proposed to her, she would assume he loved her, too, and she would expect him to act accordingly. For him to do otherwise would hurt her deeply, as would any insistence on his part that their marriage be one of convenience.

To deny the passion he'd displayed for her during their lovemaking would demean her in a way she didn't deserve. And to try to keep that passion in check while living with her as husband and wife would drive him crazy.

He would end up so madly in love with her that just the thought of losing her would tie him up in knots.

Yes, marriage was definitely out of the question.

Not that it would even prove necessary. His myriad, mind-boggling what-ifs could very well be all for naught because their one act of unprotected sexual intercourse would more than likely have no repercussions at all for either one of them.

And *should* Abby end up pregnant, Jack reminded himself, it wouldn't be *his* fault alone.

The box of condoms he had found under the sink could have expired years ago. And while he hadn't thought to check, neither had she. They had both taken an equal chance using them.

So *if,* by some fluke, a pregnancy did result, Abby would have to be the one to decide what she wanted to do about it. Whether or not to include him in her decision would be her choice, as well.

He would give her all the help he could—at a distance, as a friend. And though he would miss being a part of the child's life, the other alternative—taking on the responsibilities of husband and father, with all the emotional involvement that would entail—was strictly out of the question.

He had barely survived losing Cindy. He wasn't about to set himself up for other, equally devastating losses when he'd gotten by on his own just fine the past few years.

His mind made up, Jack finally eased out of Abby's bed again. Carefully, he pulled the quilt up around her shoulders, then couldn't resist the urge to feather a last, light kiss on her velvety cheek. To his relief, she barely stirred, but the room had grown light enough for him to see the faint smile that turned up the corners of her mouth.

His body responded with a speed and intensity that nearly knocked his knees out from under him. Only by reminding himself of the trouble he had already caused them both did he find the strength to turn away from her.

In the bathroom once more, he dressed quickly, then made his way to the kitchen where he found paper and a pen in one of the drawers.

He wrote quickly—just the bare facts—included his telephone number in Houston as well as his parents' telephone number in Promise, and signed his name with a flourish. He propped the note against the salt-and-pepper shakers on the table so Abby would be sure to see it, then collected his coat from the hallway and let himself out the front door.

Already the sky had begun to turn a pale pink on the eastern horizon. Without glancing at his watch, Jack knew it was after six. He would have barely enough time to get home, pack his suitcase and make the drive to Las Vegas to catch his nine o'clock flight to Houston. Gratefully, he noted that at least the weather had cleared overnight.

He was almost to his rental car when he saw the elderly woman, bundled up in a fuzzy robe, walking a tiny, equally aged white poodle along the swatch of grass that edged the driveway. Startled, he hesitated a moment, uncertain what to say to her, if anything.

The woman stared back at him with obvious interest, an avid gleam in her eyes, then spoke in a surprisingly strong voice considering her small stature.

"You're the Randalls' boy, aren't you? Don't suppose you remember me. I worked at your father's bank up until five years ago when I retired. Constance Beckworth is my name." She paused for half a beat, only giving Jack time to nod and smile in feigned recognition. Then she added with a malicious grin, ''I thought I'd seen the last of the overnight *guests* slipping out of that house at dawn when the Summers woman passed away a few days ago. But it looks like the apple didn't fall far from the tree…if you get my drift. I'd be careful, though…a nice young man like you. You don't want to get yourself tied up with the likes of *them*.''

Jack's smile froze on his face as he realized what the old woman was insinuating about Abby…*his* Abby. Outrage on her behalf warred with a full measure of shame for opening her up to the gossipmongering that would surely follow this unfortunate incident.

He had no doubt Constance Beckworth would see to it that news of Abby's overnight *guest* was spread all over town, and there wasn't much he could do to stop her.

Leveling a stern gaze the woman's way, Jack said, ''Don't believe everything you see, Mrs. Beckworth. Abby's just a friend. A good friend who recently lost her mother. I would hope you'd be more interested in offering her a little sympathy rather than talking about her so unkindly.''

Mrs. Beckworth turned away from him with a derisive sniff, letting him know exactly what she thought of *that* idea, then called to her little dog.

Cursing her as well as himself, Jack ducked into his car and started the engine. Never in a million years had he intended to cause Abby so many problems, but it seemed that was exactly what he'd done.

He had been so damned determined to take care of *his* wants and needs that he hadn't even begun to consider the possible consequences Abby would have to face. And here he was, running away like a callous bastard, leaving her to fend for herself.

The alternative scared him half out of his wits, though.

Which made him a *cowardly* callous bastard...

Jack had never thought of himself as being perfect—far from it, in fact. He had his faults just like everyone else. Yet he had always considered himself to be one of the good guys.

Driving away from Abby Summers' mother's house that cold December morning, however, he felt anything but good about himself. And he knew, in his heart, that it was going to be a very long time before he ever would again.

Chapter Seven

When Abby first awoke, she knew at once that she'd slept much longer than she should have. Sunlight teased around the edges of the blinds on the window above her bed, a sure sign that the day was already well underway. And even before she shifted from her side to her back, she also knew that she was alone.

Gazing longingly at the empty place beside her that Jack had filled with his gloriously masculine presence during the night, she suffered a pang of regret.

Not for what she had done. Making love with Jack Randall had been truly wondrous, a magical experience unlike any she'd had in the past, or would have with anyone but him in the future. His passion for her had freed her own carefully controlled, long-concealed emotions, revealing the true depth of intimacy a man and woman in love could share.

How she would have treasured greeting this glorious morning in his arms—the first of many they'd have together, she was sure.

But she was being greedy, not to mention wholly self-centered.

According to the clock on the nightstand, it was already after seven. Hadn't Jack told her that his flight back to Houston left early today? He had probably wanted to shower, dress and drink a cup of coffee before he returned to his parents' house to pack.

Sure that he must be in the kitchen, Abby scrambled out of bed and crossed to the closet to retrieve her cozy, white terry-cloth robe. Bundling into it, she went to join him. They wouldn't have much of a chance to talk before he would have to leave, but words weren't really necessary after last night.

She'd settle for a hug and one, maybe two, of his thoroughly luscious kisses to tide her over until they could be together again. And they could decide when that would be over the phone once they were both home again that evening. They'd have more than enough time then, to plan—

As Abby halted in the kitchen doorway, she saw immediately that the room was empty. Frowning, she turned back the way she had come, noting that the bare Christmas tree still stood in the living room. She hadn't heard any sounds coming from the bathroom, but that was the only other place Jack could be.

Unless he'd gone outside for some reason…

She quickly discovered that Jack wasn't in the bathroom. With a glance out the front door, she saw that his rental car wasn't parked in the driveway any longer, either.

Abby was disappointed by the fact that he'd gone, but not drastically so. His flight to Houston must have been scheduled to leave Las Vegas much earlier than she had thought, and kind soul that he was, he had chosen to slip away without disturbing her.

Obviously, she had been sleeping soundly, so soundly she hadn't heard him rustling around the house, and he hadn't had the heart to wake her.

Much as she wished he had, she could understand. His intentions had been good, after all. And surely he'd left a note for her....

Abby returned to her bedroom, but didn't find one there. The kitchen, then, she thought as she crossed the living room again, her steps light and quick.

With a heart-skip of relief, she saw the single piece of paper on the table, propped up against her mother's palm tree salt-and-pepper shakers. For just a moment, she had been afraid that Jack had left without a word. She should have known he would never do that to her—not after last night.

Standing beside the table, Abby picked up Jack's note and began to read it. Then, very slowly, very carefully, she sat down on one of the chairs.

A wave of heat washed over her, followed by a feeling that made her think of a cold fist squeezing hard around her heart. Her head spun dizzily, she couldn't quite catch her breath, and the way her stomach rolled and tumbled, she thought she was going to vomit.

As one minute ticked into another on the teapot clock above the refrigerator, Abby gripped the paper in her hand and stared at nothing while she forced herself to take deep, steadying breaths. After what seemed like a very long time, she finally calmed down enough to read the note again. Just to be sure she had correctly understood Jack's meaning the first time.

Jack had written in his surprisingly legible handwriting:

Just so you know, I noticed a small tear in the condom we used the second time around. Odds are, nothing will come of it, but I wanted to warn you just in case. Please call me if a problem should develop. I will help you any way I can. It was good seeing you again. Take care.

He had signed his name and included a couple of telephone numbers, one for his apartment in Houston and another for his parents' house in Promise. Just in case a *problem* should develop.

"And what problem would that be, Jack Randall? A baby on the way?" Abby muttered, the hurt she felt at his casual dismissal of her and all she had thought they'd shared turning to anger. "Like I would ever go to you for any kind of help ever in my life, you...you...*jerk*."

It wasn't the tear in the condom that upset her so much. Odds *were* against a pregnancy resulting, considering her cycle was fairly regular and she should still be within her *safe* period.

What had her wanting to hurl crockery against the wall was realizing that she had never really known Jack Randall at all. And because she hadn't really known him, all the sharing and caring she'd read into the time they'd spent together last night had been nothing more than a figment of her imagination.

She might have thought they were making love, but to Jack they were simply having a couple of *rounds* of sex—no strings attached.

And, oh, by the way, good seeing you again this *one* time. Unless, of course, a *problem* develops.

Abby didn't even want to begin to think about what his solution to *that* would be. She was already disillusioned enough about Jack Randall to last a lifetime. There was no sense making herself really depressed.

Wadding his note into a ball, she stuffed it into the pocket of her robe, pushed away from the table and went to take a shower. Her anger stayed with her until she stood under the pounding spray of hot water. Then, despite her best intentions, she started to cry.

How could she have been so wrong about him? What cues to his true character had she missed, especially last night? She had been needy, yes, but not desperately so. She'd certainly had all her wits about her. So much so that she'd never expected the evening to end the way it had. And she couldn't remember anything off-hand about Jack's manner during the hours they'd spent together, either.

There had been several times when they could have gone their separate ways, but he had let those moments pass. He had seemed to truly want her company, and his passion for her had seemed to be both honest and intense.

Trusting in his basic decency and honor, Abby had savored every moment of their lovemaking. Foolishly, it now appeared, because there was nothing decent or honorable about the man who had written the note she'd found on her mother's kitchen table.

"So get over it," she chided herself as she dried her hair.

She'd had a very nice life before she had sex with Jack Randall, and she would continue to have a very nice life, whether or not she ever saw him again.

The telephone rang as Abby set aside her blow dryer, and she was proud of the fact that she swiftly dismissed the possibility that it could be Jack. As she fully expected when she lifted the receiver, it was her grandmother, calling to ask if she still planned to stop by for breakfast.

"Of course, I do," Abby assured her. "I'm just running a little later than I anticipated."

"Late night last night?" Judith asked, sounding quite pleased by the possibility.

"Not too late," Abby answered truthfully.

She and Jack *had* gone to bed well before midnight, but she wasn't about to share that particular detail with her grandmother.

"Did you have a nice time with your young man?"

"Dinner at the café on the square was delicious, Gran. But Jack Randall isn't my young man. He's just someone I knew years ago. I doubt we'll ever cross paths again." At least not as long as *she* had anything to say about it, Abby thought, then added briskly, "I'd better let you go so I can finish packing. I shouldn't be more than thirty minutes, forty-five at the most."

"I've got the pancake batter all ready. Your favorite, with fresh blueberries. I'll go ahead and start the bacon, too."

"Sounds good, Gran. See you in a little while."

All Abby really wanted to do was slink back to San Francisco without seeing or speaking to anyone. She couldn't disappoint her grandparents, though. Even if it meant she had to paste a cheery smile on her face and pretend that nothing out of the ordinary had happened with her *old friend,* Jack Randall.

She wasn't about to burden Judith and Hank with her heartache. Not when she had so carelessly brought it upon herself. They would stand by her, of course, just as they had always stood by Larissa. But unless she found herself in a situation where that would prove necessary—a situation, she reminded herself, that seemed highly unlikely—she planned to keep silent about how she and Jack had spent last night.

Determined to banish him from her thoughts, Abby dressed in gray wool slacks and the pale yellow cashmere sweater set Judith had given her for Christmas, then gathered her hair into a tortoiseshell clip at the base of her neck. She tucked her robe into her suitcase and shut it, made a quick survey of her bedroom, and headed for the living room.

There she once again saw the Christmas tree standing forlornly in the corner. She would have to ask Hank to stop by later and put it out on the curb for the trash pickup.

After making sure everything else was in order, she put on her coat, grabbed her purse and suitcase, and walked out to her rental car.

As she loaded the suitcase into the trunk, she saw her mother's neighbor, Constance Beckworth, lurking in the shadows on the tiny front porch of her house, her little poodle clutched in her arms.

The woman had never once spared Abby a friendly word, not even after news of Larissa's death had appeared in the local paper. Normally, Abby would have ignored her presence altogether. But that morning she was feeling just perverse enough to smile widely and wave to the woman.

"Hello, Mrs. Beckworth. Nice day, isn't it?" she called out.

Abby could almost hear Constance's dismissive snort as the old woman turned on her heel and stalked into her house, her head held high.

Just one more thing that would never change in the small town she had once called home, Abby thought as she climbed into the car.

Which was not only why she had left Promise, Nevada, in the first place, but also one of many reasons why she couldn't get back to San Francisco fast enough now.

Chapter Eight

Jack had been in San Francisco two days—two long, miserably cold, damp, rainy March days, most of which he'd spent in the quiet, upscale neighborhood where Abby lived, driving past her town house.

He'd had no trouble finding her. She had talked freely about where she worked and how close it was to where she lived, and her name and address were listed in the telephone book. All he had needed was a street map of the city, and there he had been yesterday afternoon, rolling slowly past her house. Since it had been Friday, he'd figured she was at work, so he had felt safe enough making his first foray there.

The first of what had turned out to be many attempts to work up the nerve to actually walk up to her front door, Jack thought as he sat in his rental car, parked half a block away on the gently sloping street. He knew she was home. He had seen her pull into her ground floor garage almost an hour earlier, and there were lights on in several of the front windows of the tall, narrow town house. Still, he hesitated.

He was running out of time to see her, face-to-face, to apologize for the way he'd walked out on her in December, and to ask her if maybe, just maybe, she could find it in her heart to give him a chance to make things right between them. But he was having the damnedest time convincing himself that she would open her door to him, much less listen to anything he had to tell her.

To say that he had behaved badly toward her was an understatement. None of the excuses he had made to himself since he'd walked out on her over two months ago changed that. And all of his attempts to put her out of his mind, as well as his heart, had failed, as well.

He had fallen asleep every night missing Abby terribly, and he had awakened all too many mornings from dreams so vivid that his first instinct had been to reach out for her across the empty expanse of his lonely bed.

Jack hadn't wanted to feel so deeply for any woman ever again in his life. He hadn't realized until too late that despite his best efforts to remain cool and detached, his wants and needs had gotten the better of him.

And, oh, how he had found himself wanting, *needing,* Abby Summers…

Not just for sex, but for sharing the smallest, most mundane things like buying a sack of groceries at the neighborhood market, chopping vegetables for a salad, watching a sitcom on television, drinking a glass of wine in front of a roaring fire, or taking a long walk in the early evening.

And talking…talking about everything and anything the way they'd done at dinner that night.

It was the companionship they had shared that Jack longed for as much as anything. Though he would give just about anything he possessed to make love to her again.

But he had been afraid that he had ruined whatever chance he'd had to have a deep and meaningful relationship with her when he'd treated her so callously.

Only the hope that he might somehow be able to redeem himself in her eyes had brought him to San Francisco. Unfortunately, that hope had been growing fainter and fainter as the hours passed.

He wanted to believe that Abby would at least hear him out. But he also knew that wouldn't guarantee him anything. She could still want nothing more to do with him on principle alone. Or she could have met someone else in the months they'd been apart, and nothing he said would matter to her now.

The knot that had been twisting in Jack's gut for two days tightened even more. He had been such a fool in December—such a cowardly fool. He had run from the best thing that had happened to him in years, and he had regretted it ever since.

Working up the courage to fly to San Francisco had taken him several weeks. And now, working up the courage to talk to Abby had him all but paralyzed.

"Enough," he muttered angrily, thrusting open the car door.

For two days, he hadn't been able to eat and he

hadn't been able to sleep. If he went back to Promise without resolving this situation, one way or another, for better or worse, there was no telling when he'd be good for anything again, and he simply couldn't afford that.

Not when he had yet to start pulling his weight at the clinic he'd joined a month ago.

With the cold rain pelting down on him, Jack walked purposefully to Abby's town house. He climbed the short flight of steps, stood on the small front porch and pressed the doorbell once, then again. Several moments passed during which he was grateful for the slight overhang that kept him from getting even wetter than he already was.

Finally, he heard the lock turn and the door, still on its safety chain, opened just a few inches. In the entryway light, Jack saw Abby peering out at him. She was wearing a long, wooly, hunter-green robe and his first impression was that she looked exhausted.

"Hi," he said for lack of anything better.

To his relief, she released the safety chain and opened the door a little wider, but she didn't say anything at first. Instead, she gazed at him long and hard as she straightened her shoulders. Her blue eyes flashed angrily, as well, chasing away any sign of weariness on her part.

"Well, well, well…" she said at last, her voice frosty. "If it isn't Jack Randall. What brings *you* here? Looking for another sexual *go around?* Or are you just checking to see if a *problem* has *developed?*"

"Abby, please, I just want—" he began, appalled

by just how crude the words he'd written in his note sounded now that he heard them spoken aloud.

"Sorry, Jack. Either way, you're out of luck," she continued, cutting him off in a matter-of-fact tone. "We've had all the sexual *go arounds* we're ever going to have. And you are the last person on the face of the earth I'd go to with a *problem,* even one of your making."

Before he could put out a hand to hold the door open, Abby closed it in his face. As the lock clicked into place, he beat a fist on the wood.

"Abby, wait, I have to talk to you," he shouted. "I made a big mistake and I'm sorry, so very, very sorry."

"We both made a big mistake, and believe me, I'm just as sorry as you are. As for talking, the time for that is long past."

"But, Abby, you don't understand. When I said I made a mistake I didn't mean—"

"Go away, Jack." Again she cut him off decisively. "Go away right now or I'm calling the police."

He stood on the porch for a few moments more, too stunned by her flat refusal to listen to anything he had to say to move away. He had factored in such a possibility, but he hadn't really thought he'd have to deal with it.

He had told himself over and over that she would hear him out—for old times' sake, if nothing else. Once again, he had misjudged her, and in doing so, he'd blown the one chance he had to make things right between them.

Finally, Jack made himself turn and walk down the steps. He couldn't force her to listen to him, and he certainly didn't want to cause her any further distress. He'd obviously hurt her badly, and he couldn't blame her for not wanting anything more to do with him.

He could only blame himself and his stupidity, and he could only do that for so long. Then he was going to have to accept, once and for all, that he was better off alone, and get on with his life again as best he could. Either that, or try to think of another way to win back her regard.

Deciding, one way or another, would have to wait until tomorrow, though. Tonight he was going to find a liquor store, buy a bottle of bourbon, go back to his hotel room and have himself a little pity party. There would be hell to pay in the morning, but anything that took his mind off Abby Summers, even temporarily, would be worth it in the end.

Chapter Nine

Abby huddled on the entryway floor, her back pressed against the solid wood of the door listening to the sound of Jack's footsteps as he left her front porch. The pounding beat of her heart finally began to slow, but her anger lingered on.

How dare he show up out of nowhere, expecting her to listen to his excuses? And to do so now, of all times.

Was it merely coincidence that Jack had come to San Francisco just days after her doctor confirmed that she was pregnant? Or had Judith taken it upon herself to share the news with him despite her granddaughter's insistence that there was no need for him to know?

When Abby had called to tell her about the baby, admitting at the same time that she and Jack had shared more than dinner in December, Gran had said it was only fair that he be advised of the situation, as well. In Judith's eyes, Jack was an honorable man, and she'd been sure that once he knew Abby was carrying his child, he would do right by her. They had obviously cared enough about each other to make love, and as far as her grandmother was concerned, they would have as much chance as any couple to live happily-ever-after with that foundation to build on.

Abby hadn't wanted to disillusion Judith by telling her exactly how Jack had viewed their one night of intimacy, but neither was she going to accept charity of any kind from him just to relieve her grandmother's anxiety.

She wasn't like Larissa. She had a high-paying job, a home of her own, and enough savings to see her through the weeks of maternity leave she would be taking. She didn't need a man around to take care of her, even temporarily. And she certainly didn't need a man telling her what she should do about her *problem.* To her way of thinking, she didn't have one.

From the moment her doctor had confirmed her suspicions, Abby realized just how much she wanted the child growing in her womb. In fact, her maternal instincts had risen with a fierceness that had taken her by surprise. She would have to keep on working, as most single mothers did, but she was already planning to spend every free hour she had with her baby.

Her baby, created in a moment when *her* heart, at least, had been filled with the glory and wonder of love.

Had their night together meant as much to Jack, Abby would have gone to him with her news in an instant. But he'd let her know it hadn't. With that in mind, she'd decided it would be better to raise her child alone. She didn't want her son or daughter to ever be treated like an unwanted burden.

She had managed just fine without a father, thanks in large part to Judith and Hank, and they would be there for her child, too, albeit at a distance.

Unless she could find a way of talking them into moving to San Francisco.

Abby had plenty of room for them, as well as the baby, in her town house. And with her grandparents living in San Francisco, she would have no reason to return to Promise, Nevada once her mother's house was sold.

That would eliminate any chance of running into Jack when she had the baby in tow, and, in turn, would make her life so much easier in the long run. She didn't want him feeling obliged to her in any way, especially out of a false sense of responsibility.

Having come full circle, Abby found herself wondering, once again, whether Jack had come to San Francisco because Judith told him about her pregnancy. Aware that there was only one way to find out, she got to her feet rather gracelessly and went into the kitchen to call her grandmother.

Judith answered after several rings, sounding sleepy.

"Hi, Gran," Abby began, hoping she hadn't awakened her grandparents. Though it was still early by her standards, she realized, too late, that they might have already gone to bed. "I hope I didn't get you up."

"Actually, your granddad and I were just getting ready to turn off the light. How are you, sweetie?"

"Just fine, Gran."

"Still feeling sick in the morning?"

"Yes, but it doesn't seem quite as bad now that I know the reason for it."

"You're probably over the worst of it," Judith said, her tone reassuring.

"Probably," Abby agreed, then hesitated.

Maybe she should wait to tell her grandmother about Jack's visit. She didn't want to cause her unnecessary concern so close to bedtime. Still, the sooner she knew if *he* knew about the baby, the better prepared she would be for any further salvos on his part.

Jack might not care about *her,* but he might care enough about his child to demand custody rights. That could open up a whole new, potentially devastating, can of worms. The Randalls were rich and powerful people, used to getting what they wanted. And if they wanted her child…

"I had a visitor earlier this evening," Abby said, willing away the small knot of fear that had settled in her stomach. "Jack Randall came to see me. I was wondering if you…if you sent him here."

"Oh, no, Abby. I would never do that. At least, not knowing how you feel about the situation. I might not agree with you, but I've respected your wishes."

"Thanks, Gran. I really appreciate it."

So, Jack hadn't come out of sense of responsibility or out of a need to establish his parental rights, Abby thought with relief. But then, why had he made the effort to track her down?

Her grandmother seemed to be thinking along the same lines.

"He must have really wanted to see you to take time away from the clinic when he's only been working there a month or so," Judith said, her tone brightening considerably. "What did he say? And, more importantly, what did *you* say?"

"He said he wanted to talk to me," Abby replied. "I told him the time for talking had long passed, and then I sent him away."

"Oh, Abby, you didn't," Judith murmured, making no effort to hide her dismay.

Of course, her grandmother wasn't aware of how he'd left her that cold December morning—with a bare-facts note about a torn condom. But Judith's comment made Abby realize that she might have made a mistake when she refused to hear what Jack had to say.

"What should I have done instead?" she asked, allowing her frustration to get the better of her. "Invite him to have a drink, listen quietly to whatever he wanted to tell me, then casually mention that I'm expecting his baby?"

"And what would have been so wrong about that?" her grandmother asked, in turn.

"I don't want his charity," Abby said.

"Maybe charity isn't what he would have offered you."

Abby couldn't bring herself to admit that her grandmother might be right. Instead, she stated as breezily as she could, "He was just a friend. A friend who happened to be feeling sad and lonely at the same time I was. We spent a night together, and that's all there is to it."

Judith didn't say anything for several moments,

then finally conceded, ''Well, dear, you know him better than I do.''

Abby wasn't sure how true that was, but she wasn't about to admit it. After promising to call again in a few days, she said goodbye to her grandmother and cradled the receiver.

The rest of the evening stretched ahead of her, long and lonely. She couldn't seem to settle down to anything, especially the work she'd brought home from the office. She drifted from room to room, picking up a book, then setting it down, turning on the television, clicking through the channels, then turning it off again. And all the time she thought about Jack, wondering where he was and what he was doing, then telling herself she didn't care.

She didn't want him in her life, and she certainly didn't need him in it, either. Just because he'd had an attack of conscience about the way he'd left her in December—which had to be why he'd come to San Francisco—didn't mean she had to beat herself up for sending him away so rudely.

Still, Abby kept catching herself playing what-if.

What if he had come to see her because he'd realized he loved her? What if the mistake he said he'd made had been walking out on her? What if he had wanted to make up for the hurtful way he'd treated her? If only she hadn't reacted out of anger and, in all honesty, fear, as well.

If only she had given him a chance to say what was on his mind. Maybe she wouldn't be alone tonight, after all.

Or maybe she would be even more alone than ever....

Better not to have any more hopes or dreams that

revolved around Jack Randall, Abby cautioned herself as she finally crawled into bed.

Having them dashed once had been more than enough for her.

Chapter Ten

Jack finished dictating notes on his morning patients into his recorder for the clinic secretary to transcribe, then glanced at his watch and checked his schedule for the afternoon. He had over an hour before his next patient was due—time enough to walk over to the café across the square and eat a sandwich. Better yet, he could order something to go, then stop in at the real estate agent's office to check on the progress of his loan application and the results of the inspection on the house just outside of town that he had finally decided to buy.

Getting approval for the loan shouldn't be a problem, as the agent had assured him. Even though he had only been working at the clinic three months and his salary was relatively modest, he didn't have any other debts.

He also knew that the old, ranch-style house on

several acres of land that included a small orchard needed work, most of which he planned to do himself. The inspection was mainly to determine that the foundation was solid, the roof wouldn't cave in, and the plumbing and electrical wiring would suffice for a while without the risk of pipes bursting or lights shorting out.

His parents had wanted him to buy one of the two much more elegant houses currently on the market in their exclusive neighborhood—a home more befitting his position, his mother had said. Jack had known that would lead, inevitably, to his being drawn into Promise's social whirl, such as it was— something he was determined to avoid at all cost.

As it was, since he'd been back in town, he had joined his parents once a month for dinner at their country club, and each time he'd been forced to extricate himself from the overly attentive company of someone's single daughter, sister, niece or cousin, twice removed.

He wasn't interested in dating anyone, even occasionally, much less pursuing a more permanent relationship. The woman he wanted didn't seem to want him, but he was far from giving up hope where she was concerned.

At the risk of looking like a stalker, Jack intended to go back to San Francisco to see Abby again over the holiday weekend at the end of May. Try as he might, he couldn't get her out of his mind. Nor would he accept that she wanted nothing more to do with him. At least not until she'd heard what he had to say about how he'd really felt the night they'd spent together in December.

Just a few more weeks, and he would be with her

again. And he would find a way to make her listen to him, no matter how he had to beg and plead. In the meantime, he planned to pour all of his excess energy into remodelling his new home, and if that made him seem antisocial, then so be it.

Pushing away from his desk, Jack stood, stacked the files for his afternoon patients that his nurse had left for his review and put them in his out box. Then he headed down the narrow hallway leading from the doctors' private offices to the clinic's back exit.

As he reached the door, it opened and one of his colleagues, the clinic's internist, Aaron Post, stepped into the hallway.

"Whew, it's hot out there and it's only the first week in May," Aaron said. Running a hand through his short, dark hair, he offered Jack a congenial smile. "You just getting away for lunch?"

"I had some notes to dictate," Jack answered by way of explanation. "I have a pretty busy afternoon ahead of me, so I thought I'd better get them done while I had the chance."

"Everything going okay?"

"So far, so good. How about you?"

"Better than good." Aaron's smile widened enigmatically.

"Hey, what's going on?" Jack asked, smiling, too.

As the staff pediatrician, he worked more closely with Donald Brooks, the clinic's OB-GYN. But he had more in common with Aaron. They were nearer in age and they were both single. Recently, they had played a couple of rounds of golf at the country club and occasionally they'd had a beer together at one of the country-western bars that Aaron patronized.

Having gone through a bitter divorce nearly two

years ago, Aaron was no more interested in dating than Jack—at least, not until lately. About three weeks ago, he'd declared that he was ready to get back in the saddle again. Since then, he'd been scoping out Promise's eligible women with increasing dedication.

Jack had declined his offer to join the hunt. In fact, he had gone so far as to introduce Aaron to his mother in the hope that she would busy herself finding *him* a mate, and thus, have no time left to meddle in her own son's life.

"I probably shouldn't tell you, but since you've said you're not interested in dating, I'm assuming you won't offer any competition," Aaron replied.

"Ah, you've met someone who measures up to your standards." Jack cocked an eyebrow inquiringly. "Who's the lucky lady?"

"I don't know her name yet. In fact, all I really know is that she's new in town. Well, not exactly *new*. She used to live here years ago, and she's come back to take care of some family business. At least according to Marilyn, our favorite waitress at the café. I'm assuming she would know since she seems to be as tapped into Promise's information pipeline as anyone around town. Oh, and she's gorgeous. Not Marilyn." Aaron rolled his eyes at the thought of plain, sturdy, old Marilyn Mertz, then added, "She has the most beautiful auburn hair, brilliant blue eyes, and one of the sweetest smiles I've ever seen."

"Where did you see her?" Jack asked, all trace of his own smile gone.

Though he could be mistaken, there was a better than average chance that the woman who had attracted Aaron's attention was Abby Summers—*his*

Abby Summers. And if she was back in Promise, for whatever reason—

"Oh, no, you don't," Aaron retorted good-naturedly. "I've got first dibs on her."

"Actually, I'm pretty sure I know who you're talking about. We went to high school together, and I saw her again when I was here in December. She's also the reason I went to San Francisco in March." Jack hesitated, then added boldly, staking his claim with a series of white lies he hoped he wouldn't regret, "I've been expecting her to show up in Promise any day now, but she loves surprises. Which is probably why I haven't seen her yet, myself."

"Just my luck...the one woman who really intrigues me, and she's already hooked up with you. No wonder you haven't been interested in dating."

"So, where did you see her?" Jack prodded, refusing to be diverted. "Maybe I can surprise *her*."

"She was sitting at one of the tables in the café, having lunch. According to Marilyn, she had an appointment with Jan Nelson at the real estate agency that had to be rescheduled for the afternoon—something to do with selling her mother's house. That Marilyn...she sure knows how to get information out of people, doesn't she?"

"Was she still at the café when you left?" Jack asked.

"She was, along with Jan Nelson, but I gathered—from Marilyn, of course—that they would be going back to Jan's office shortly. I imagine that's where you'll find her now."

"Thanks, Aaron. I owe you one."

"Big time," his friend shot back. "So, you're off to the real estate agency, then?"

Jack nodded as he moved purposefully to the door.

Oh, yes, he was going to the real estate agency. And if Abby wasn't there, he was going to her mother's house as soon as he'd seen the last of his afternoon patients. Should it be necessary, he would even go so far as to track her down at her grandparents' apartment.

"I hope she won't be upset that she didn't have a chance to surprise you," Aaron added.

"I'm sure she won't," Jack assured him with a wave of his hand.

Especially since she'd probably had no intention at all of seeing him if she could help it.

How long had she been in Promise? Jack wondered as he pushed through the door. And, more important, how long did she plan to stay?

Something told him the clock was already ticking fast. Abby wouldn't want to spend any more time in Promise than absolutely necessary, and that meant he might only have a matter of *days* to woo her into trusting him again. Just getting her to listen to him was going to take some doing. Getting her to believe in him again as well would be even more difficult. She would have only his word to go on. And he would be contradicting what he'd written in that damned note....

But why would he pursue her unless he truly cared for her? He would have to make a point of asking her just that question, he decided. She had closed her door in his face once. Only a man deeply in love would try again to prove himself worthy.

She wouldn't be able to argue with that bit of reasoning, and that, in turn, would surely work in his favor.

Outside the clinic, the midday heat hit Jack full force, the bright sunlight making him squint. He fished his sunglasses from his shirt pocket and slipped them on as he walked up the side street that led to the town square.

He cut across the little park, grateful for the patches of shade provided by the trees, barely acknowledging the greetings of the few people he passed. He kept his gaze focused on the real estate agency's tidy storefront window, willing Abby to still be there.

Since he could claim to have legitimate business with Jan Nelson, himself, he would be able to make their meeting seem accidental. And with other people around, Abby's anger at him might not flare up quite as wildly as it had in San Francisco.

That would give him the opening he needed to talk to her in a calm and sensible manner. Then he could finally set things right between them. And they could start thinking about the future, and how they wanted to spend it together.

Chapter Eleven

Abby sat in front of Jan Nelson's desk, waiting as patiently as she could for the real estate agent to check over the papers Abby had signed granting Jan's agency the right to list her mother's house for sale.

She had expected to be finished with the whole business much sooner, but Jan had been busy with another client when she arrived for her appointment. Apologizing profusely, the agent had suggested that Abby might want to grab a bite to eat at the café rather than spend the "hour, at the most" in the agency's waiting room.

It had been close enough to lunch time, and as seemed to be the case more often than not lately, Abby had been hungry. So she had agreed, reluctantly risking the possibility that she'd run into Jack

Randall at the very place where they'd had dinner in December.

Odds were that she'd cross paths with him sometime during her planned three-week stay in Promise, but she would rather not do it on her second day in town. The second-to-*last* day would be much easier to handle.

Jan had joined her just as she'd finished her chicken salad sandwich, and had insisted on picking up the tab. Back at her office, she had also readily agreed to Abby's request that she handle all the details necessary to ensure the speediest possible sale of Larissa's house.

She had used the demands of her job as the reason why she would rather not have to return to Promise to oversee the process herself. But she suspected the agent knew that her pregnancy was a factor, as well.

While Abby's condition wasn't all that obvious yet, especially in the loose-fitting dresses she planned to wear while she was in town, a woman with eyes as discerning as Jan Nelson would have known she was pregnant almost immediately. The agent had to have also noticed that Abby wasn't wearing a wedding ring, and she hadn't mentioned a partner of any kind, either.

Small-town resident that she'd been all her life, Jan had surely realized that Abby would prefer to stir up as little gossip as possible. And that could only be accomplished if she managed to stay away from Promise, Nevada once her girth had begun to expand.

Which was exactly what Abby hoped to be able to do with the agent's help.

"Well, everything seems to be in order," Jan said at last, smiling as she glanced at Abby. "Let me make a copy of the paperwork for you. Then we can decide on a time when I can stop by to take a few photographs for the multiple listings and the ad I'll run in the paper. I'd also like to walk through the house so I can make sure we haven't missed any important selling points.''

''Fine,'' Abby agreed, stifling a sigh of exasperation as the woman pushed away from her desk and walked briskly out of the office.

She wanted to go back to her mother's house, close the blinds, crawl into bed and sleep the rest of the afternoon away, safe from prying eyes and whispering tongues. But she had to stop by her grandparents' apartment to tell them about her meeting with the real estate agent, and then the grocery store to buy some fresh fruit and vegetables, milk, juice, bread, cereal, fish, chicken—

Abby's stomach growled, making her smile. She had just eaten lunch, and she was already thinking about dinner tonight, not to mention breakfast tomorrow. She was going to weigh a ton by the time the baby came. But that was all right as long as he or she was healthy, she thought, resting a hand protectively on her tummy.

In response, she felt the faintest flutter deep inside her womb, like a butterfly spreading its wings, then taking flight, and her smile widened. She had first experienced the sensation a couple of weeks ago, and though it now happened on a daily basis, often several times, her baby's movement still filled her with a sense of awe.

Her baby...her precious baby...tumbling around inside her with strength and spirit, reassuring Abby that bringing her child into the world had been the right choice. A choice she had made on her own, and would never regret no matter what happened in the future.

Again, Abby considered the probability that she would run into Jack at least once in the next three weeks. Her grandmother had told her he was one of the physicians on staff at the clinic located right there in the town square. And though she wouldn't have much reason to be in that part of town while she was in Promise, she couldn't avoid the area altogether.

There were only so many places where she could shop for necessities, too. Places that Jack would surely frequent, as well. But maybe if she timed her forays outside her mother's house carefully enough, she would be safe.

Frowning, Abby picked at the fabric of her bright yellow sundress. *Safe*… What an odd word to use in relation to Jack Randall. As if he might cause her harm should they happen to meet.

She knew full well that he wouldn't—at least not physical harm. And any emotional turmoil she experienced would be as much her fault as his. He could only hurt her feelings if she gave him the power to do it, and she wasn't about to put herself in that position again.

Which was why she had flatly refused to even consider her grandmother's gently offered suggestion that she go to see him and tell him—

"Here you go. One copy of your agreement with the agency covering the listing and sale of your mother's house." Jan Nelson bustled back into the office, interrupting Abby's reverie. The agent handed her a file folder containing the paperwork, then sat behind her desk again and opened her appointment book. "Now, let's see if I'm free anytime tomorrow," she continued. "Yes, in the morning from eight-thirty until nine-thirty. Or, if that's too early for you, I could stop by late in the afternoon, say sometime after four, four-thirty at the latest."

"Morning would be all right," Abby said. "That way, I can start making arrangements for someone to take care of whatever needs to be done cosmetically to make the house more saleable."

"Good thinking," Jan agreed, writing Abby's name in the eight-thirty slot. "Although from what you've told me, I doubt we'll come across any major problems. You've already said you're going to give the house a thorough cleaning, and you've had a lawn service taking care of the yard." Jan hesitated a moment, a tiny frown furrowing her high forehead. "You *are* planning on leaving most of the furniture in the house until it's sold, aren't you? It will show much better if it looks lived in."

"Yes, I had planned to do that," Abby assured her.

"Good." Jan smiled once again as she nodded her approval, then stood to indicate their business was finally finished for the day.

Abby stood gratefully, as well, and extended her hand across the desk. "Thanks, Mrs. Nelson. I really appreciate all your help. And thanks again for lunch."

"Oh, my pleasure, Ms. Summers. You were so understanding about the delay. And, please, call me Jan."

"And I'm Abby."

"Abby." The agent shook her hand, her grip firm. "I'll see you tomorrow morning…without delay."

Although Abby could have just as easily seen herself out, Jan escorted her the short distance down the hallway to the reception area. Busy trying to adjust the shoulder strap of her purse while hanging onto the file folder the agent had given her, Abby walked along beside the woman, her head down.

As she entered the reception area, however, a sudden movement off to one side drew her attention as someone rose from one of the chairs. Only he wasn't just *someone,* Abby thought with sudden dismay, freezing in her tracks and causing Jan Nelson to crash into her.

The man looming tall and broad-shouldered in all his green-eyed, blond-haired, chiseled-chin glory was none other than Jack Randall. And he was eyeing her with intensity, the expression on his handsome face such an odd mix of anger and relief that her breath caught in her throat.

Instinctively, Abby put a protective hand on the gently rounded mound of her belly. Then, as Jack's gaze followed her movement, she realized her mistake and snatched it away—too late, if the way his eyes narrowed when he looked up again was any indication.

Beside her, Jan Nelson touched her shoulder apologetically. "I'm sorry, Abby. I didn't mean to bump into you like that," she murmured. Then, turning her attention to Jack, she stepped past Abby and extended her hand to him as she continued in a brighter, more syrupy tone. "Hello, Dr. Randall. Did you have an appointment with us today?" She glanced at the receptionist, busy typing at her desk. "Sheila, you should have let me know Dr. Randall was waiting."

"Actually, I'm not here to see you," Jack answered, his gaze still on Abby. "I came to meet Ms. Summers." Closing the short distance between them, he took her by the arm, his grip just firm enough that she couldn't break away without a noticeable effort, and flashing an utterly charming smile that didn't quite make it to his glinting eyes. "Abby, *darling,*" he said as he drew her toward the door. "All finished here?"

Abby stared back at him, then nodded mutely when he gave her arm a warning squeeze. Though she tried to hang back, he tugged her gently, yet purposefully, toward the door.

"I didn't know you two were...acquainted," Jan said as she hovered close.

"Oh, we're much more than friends, aren't we, *darling?*" Jack replied as he finally managed to hustle her onto the sidewalk. "I'll be in touch about the loan application and the inspection results in the next day or so."

"Of course," Jan chirped.

Jack closed the door on the woman's cheery smile, then drew Abby into a patch of shade several yards away, for which she was momentarily grateful. The combination of bright sunlight and dry heat after the hour or more she had spent in the cool, dim confines of the real estate agency, had made her feel slightly dizzy. And now, of all times, she had to have her wits about her.

Gathering every ounce of courage she possessed, Abby forced herself to look up at Jack and smile blithely.

"How nice to see you again," she chattered inanely, pretending for all she was worth that they were merely two acquaintances catching up on old times.

"My grandmother told me you had come back to Promise to join the clinic. I hope it's worked out as well as you—"

"Stop," Jack muttered, cutting her off.

Her smile fading, Abby looked away. Somehow he had known she was back in Promise. In fact, he'd known exactly where to find her. She had no idea *how*. Not that it really mattered—spooky as it was. The bottom line remained the same. By his choice, they were together now, right in the center of town. And short of creating a major scene, she couldn't escape the coming showdown.

At least the worst would have happened, she consoled herself as she waited for him to say his piece. She wouldn't have the prospect of it hanging over her head in the days ahead, and for that she could be glad.

Still holding onto Abby's arm, Jack reached out with his free hand and touched her cheek, turning her face so that she was forced to meet his gaze again.

"We have to talk," he said, his tone now soft and coaxing. "But not here."

"No, we don't," Abby insisted, trying desperately not to let down her guard.

She had forgotten just how fatal her attraction to Jack Randall could be. Standing close to him on the shady patch of sidewalk, with the touch of his hands on her suddenly warm and tender, her longing for him rose up unbidden, threatening to undermine the staunchness of her determination.

"Oh, yes we do." Holding her gaze, he shifted his hand from her face to her belly, splaying his long, clever fingers over her in a gently possessive caress.

Abby shivered delicately as a wave of heat radiated through her from her very core. Immediately, Jack took his hand away, and at the same time, he finally released his hold on her arm.

"Tonight. Seven o'clock. Your mother's house. Be there, or I swear to God I'll find you—" He stopped himself short, shoved a hand through his hair and looked down at the ground for a long moment.

He was right, Abby admitted. They had to talk, no matter how much she would prefer not to. And the sooner she assured him that she expected nothing of him, the better for both of them. They could each get on with their lives with no hard feelings between them.

Tentatively, she laid a hand on Jack's arm. When he glanced at her, she mustered a slight smile.

"I'll be there, Jack. I promise. And I'll listen to whatever you have to say if you'll promise to listen to me, too."

He eyed her silently a few seconds longer, then smiled sheepishly.

"It's a deal," he said. Then, before she had time to realize what he had in mind, he put his hands on her shoulders, pulled her close, and kissed her, hard, on the mouth.

Giving her no chance to protest his high-handedness, he turned and walked away as Abby stood on the sidewalk, lips parted, staring at his back. Only the murmur of voices and a little girl's giggle brought her back down to earth.

Great, just *great,* she thought as she turned in the opposite direction to retrieve her rental car from the nearby parking lot. Home a couple of days, and already she had made a spectacle of herself with Jack

Randall in the town square. The telephone lines would be buzzing the rest of the afternoon.

But that was all right. She wouldn't be around long enough to let the gossip bother her. And the Randalls were so well-liked and admired that they wouldn't be affected at all.

So their son had kissed one of the town's least favored former residents. Such an outrageous action would only make him that much more interesting to Promise's eligible young debutantes—any one of whom he could, and probably would, have as his wife within the year. And that was fine with Abby. Just fine and dandy.

Or so she tried to tell herself as the afternoon hours crawled slowly by.

She stopped to see her grandparents so she could tell them she'd listed Larissa's house with Jan Nelson's real estate agency, but she studiously avoided any mention of her subsequent meeting with Jack. Then she shopped for groceries, and home again, started cleaning out the kitchen pantry, looking at the clock on the wall so many times it got to be ridiculous.

Finally, so tired she could hardly keep her eyes open, she stripped off her dress and crawled into her narrow bed. She would sleep just one hour. That would give her time to shower, put on a clean dress and freshen her makeup before Jack arrived. Thus bolstered, she would be able to face him with enough equanimity to avoid letting her true feelings show.

She didn't want him thinking he owed her anything just because she was pregnant. Because he didn't. And she didn't want him thinking she would take his charity. Because she wouldn't.

She wasn't like Larissa. She didn't measure her feelings of self-worth by a man's interest in her, especially an interest born out of a sense of duty. Jack hadn't loved her in December, and no matter what he said, she knew he couldn't possibly love her now. He was feeling guilty, as he had been in March. And a relationship born of culpability was the last thing she wanted or needed.

She would much rather take care of herself and her baby on her own, and she had every intention of making sure Jack understood that before they parted company, once and for all.

Chapter Twelve

Consummate professional that he was, Jack managed to get through the rest of the afternoon without doing any disservice to his young patients. He had willingly taken on the responsibility for their care, so he had to give their needs top priority.

But thoughts of Abby were never far from his mind—thoughts that triggered a whole gamut of emotions from anger and confusion that she hadn't told him about her pregnancy as soon as she'd known, to elation that she was here in Promise.

In her current condition, surely she would now be willing to let him make things right between them.

With each child he saw during his hours at the clinic, Jack was also reminded that he would soon have a son or daughter of his own. That realization brought with it warring emotions, as well—a great deal of pride in the family he had started, tempered with a full measure of fear at all he once again had to lose.

As an only child, he had missed having brothers and sisters, and the same had been true of Cindy. They had planned to have a houseful of children once Jack finished medical school. Then Cindy had died, and Jack had lost all desire to offer fate another hostage.

He hadn't counted on how he would feel when he saw Abby Summers that cold, lonely night in December. Nor had he expected that the life force within him—tamped down for so long—would rear its wild and crazy head.

Jack had made love to Abby with an uncontrolled passion unlike any he had ever experienced. How right it now seemed that a child had been conceived during those wondrous moments. And how doubly foolish of him to think that running away would save him from pain.

He hadn't had a moment of real peace since he'd walked out on Abby, and he wouldn't until he made her and their child a permanent part of his life. Instead of isolating himself behind the heartachingly lonely walls of his fear as he had for too many years already, he would take each day as it came, enjoy his time with Abby and the baby to the fullest, and put worst case scenarios out of his mind altogether.

With only an hour to spare until he was due at Abby's mother's house, Jack left the clinic and drove the short distance to the small apartment he had rented in lieu of moving in with his parents until he was able to buy a house of his own.

His mother had considered it a waste of money, but hadn't given him any grief once he'd made up his mind. She had probably concluded that he would be more likely to date, and thus eventually provide her with a new daughter-in-law if he had a place of his own.

Jack couldn't help but smile when he thought of how surprised and pleased she and his father would be when he told them about Abby. Especially since they had begun to despair of ever having grandchildren to spoil.

He and Abby might not have gone the more traditional route of marrying first, but Jack knew his parents would welcome her into the Randall family with the same love and affection they had always offered him. They had taught him to be a kind and decent person by their example, and he had no doubt that their kindness and decency would be extended to anyone with whom he chose to share his life.

And Abby Summers wasn't just anyone. She was one very special lady.

After a quick shower, Jack dressed in tailored navy blue shorts and a green knit polo shirt that he'd been told almost matched his eyes, slipped his feet into leather deck shoes and grabbed his car keys. He would be a little early, but he'd rather that than keep Abby waiting.

He hadn't been his most personable self on the sidewalk outside the real estate agency. Of course, he'd been in a mild state of shock from the moment Abby had rested her hand on her belly, revealing, apparently unintentionally, her pregnancy. And he had been afraid that she would try to shut him out again.

He had spent the two months since his trip to San Francisco cursing himself for not being more forceful with her that stormy night. He hadn't wanted to make the same mistake again. But neither had he meant to bully her.

Jack didn't think he had—at least not hurtfully so. But just in case his way needed smoothing, he stopped at a flower shop that was just about to close, and bought a bunch of pink-and-white carnations tucked in a paper cone with feathery greenery and sprigs of something the florist called baby's breath that seemed suitable for the occasion.

He was relieved to see a car parked in the driveway when he finally reached Abby's mother's house. With an equal measure of dismay, he also noted that meddling old Mrs. Beckworth was standing on her front lawn, paying more attention to his arrival than to the little poodle snuffling around in the bushes.

Jack would have preferred not to acknowledge the woman's presence, but as he climbed out of his car, she called out to him in her high-pitched, busybody-on-duty voice.

"Well, it's you again, young Master Randall. Thought you would have more sense than to sniff around that house again, coming from such an important family and being a professional man yourself. I suppose that's not enough to keep you from thinking with the wrong part of your anatomy, though. If you get my drift…"

Jack did, only too well, but he refused to give Constance Beckworth even the slightest bit of satisfaction by letting her know it.

"Why, good evening to you, Mrs. Beckworth," he said instead. "Enjoying the nice weather we've been having?"

The old woman looked at him through narrowed

eyes, her lips pursed disapprovingly. Holding the paper cone of flowers he'd bought for Abby, he offered the woman his most charming smile. After another moment or two, she relented, twitching her own mouth into something vaguely resembling a smile, as well.

"Very much, thank you," she replied, then snapped her fingers at the dog as she turned away.

At Abby's front door, Jack paused, drew a steadying breath, rang the doorbell and waited...and waited. Sensing Mrs. Beckworth's avid gaze trained in his direction, he glanced at his watch, drew another breath, rang the bell again, then rapped sharply on the door for good measure.

Abby had said she would be there, and he had believed her. And he was neither so early nor so late that he was encroaching on any other plans she might have made. But that didn't mean a whole hell of a lot. If she honestly didn't want to see him—

The door opened slowly and Abby peered out at him questioningly, her eyes bleary and her hair hanging loose around her shoulders in a wild mass of untamed curls. She was wearing a short, silky, royal-blue robe, and she looked as if she'd just crawled out of bed.

Jack's first thought was that she'd fallen ill since he'd seen her that afternoon. Instinctively, he reached out and pressed the back of his hand to her forehead, then her cheek, checking for fever.

She blinked up at him, a startled look in her eyes, then smiled sheepishly.

"No matter how bad I look, I'm not sick," she said, taking a step back. "I decided to take a short nap, and lost track of time...."

"You don't look bad at all," Jack assured her. "But I can come back a little later, if you'd like."

He didn't really want to go. She looked so lovely with her eyes heavy-lidded with the dregs of sleep and her luscious hair all but begging to be touched. She also seemed softer and much more amenable than she had that afternoon.

Winning her over in her current state would be so much easier. He had always prided himself on being fair, though. And getting what he wanted wouldn't be nearly as satisfying if Abby later claimed that she'd been at a disadvantage.

"No, stay." She opened the door wider and gestured for him to come inside. "It will only take me a few minutes to put some clothes on and comb my hair. Why don't you help yourself to a drink? There's iced tea and orange juice in the refrigerator, and hard stuff in one of the cabinets. You remember the way to the kitchen, don't you?"

And to your bedroom, he wanted to add, but didn't.

Her whole demeanor had changed the moment he'd stepped inside the house, signaling loud and clear her wariness of him.

So much for having her at a disadvantage. Suddenly, he was afraid to say or do anything that would make her trust him even less.

"I should put these in some water, too," he said, holding up the flowers.

"Yes, please. There should be a couple of vases under the kitchen sink. The flowers are lovely, by the way. Thanks for bringing them."

She smiled slightly, but didn't quite meet his gaze before she turned away.

Jack found a suitable vase where Abby said he would, arranged the flowers in it as best he could and added water. Then he poured a glass of tea for himself. He hadn't thought to ask Abby if she wanted anything, but just in case, he filled a glass with tea for her, as well.

Juggling the glasses and the vase, he returned to the living room and set everything on the coffee table. Too nervous to sit on the sofa while he waited for Abby, he walked over to the glass-and-brass étagère and looked at the few framed photographs displayed there.

All were of Abby and her grandparents, most taken when she was a child. But there were also two graduation photos prominently situated, one from high school and the other from Stanford. Abby's mother had obviously been very proud of her daughter, and rightly so.

But single motherhood when Abby had just started to establish herself in her chosen career wouldn't have been what Larissa Summers wanted for her. She would have wanted Abby to have a loving husband to look after her and the baby.

And she was going to have that, Jack vowed silently.

"I'm ready to talk now," Abby announced, her voice soft but firm, interrupting his thoughts.

Turning, Jack saw that she stood near the sofa, and wondered how long she'd been there. She had dressed in a pale denim jumper over a white, short-sleeved T-shirt, and she'd pulled her glorious auburn hair into a ponytail fastened with a clip at the base of her neck.

She hadn't bothered with makeup, but then, she

didn't need any to look lovely. She held herself quite regally, too, her chin up and her shoulders straight. But she'd crossed her arms over her chest protectively, and as she had earlier, she refused to meet his gaze head-on.

Jack wanted nothing more than to close the distance between them, take her in his arms, and assure her that everything would be all right. But he held back, too uncertain of her response to risk getting off on the wrong foot.

He had made enough mistakes with her already. He couldn't afford to alienate her any further. Not when his future happiness depended so completely on having her be a permanent part of his life.

"Why don't we sit down?" He gestured toward the sofa.

"I'd rather stand," she replied, her chin inching up another notch.

Not good, Jack thought. Not good at all. She obviously meant their conversation to be short and to the point. And she wasn't about to lower her guard in any way while she was at it.

"But there's a lot I need to say," he insisted, trying not to let his frustration show.

"I think I can sum it up in a few words," she countered, finally looking him in the eyes. "You've seen that a *problem* has developed as a result of our having unprotected sex, and you've decided to do what you believe to be your duty and ask me to marry you. Am I right?"

"There's more to it than that, Abby. First, I don't consider your pregnancy to be a *problem*—"

"Then what kind of *problem* were you referring to in that delightful little note you left for me in

December?'' she asked, her blue eyes flashing angrily.

"Abby...please. I never should have said the things I did in that note. I never should have left you the way I did that morning—*period*," he answered, taking a step toward her.

"You might want to think that now, but when you wrote the note and left the way you did that was what you honestly and truthfully wanted to do at the time. And there was nothing wrong with being forthright, Jack. In fact, I'm really glad you were. It's kept me from having any illusions at all about my importance to you."

"Damn it, Abby, stop twisting everything around," Jack shot back, no longer able to rein in his frustration. "I made a big mistake in December, and I'm truly sorry for it. You've got to believe me."

"Oh, I do," she acknowledged in a reasonable tone. "And if it will make you feel better, I not only accept your apology, I also absolve you of any wrongdoing toward me. Now go and have a wonderful life."

"But I can't do that. Not without—"

"Doing the *honorable* thing?" she cut in calmly. "Thanks, but no thanks, Jack. I don't need your charity."

"I didn't come here to ask you to marry me because I wanted to do a good deed," he all but shouted, desperate for a way to make her listen to him, really *listen* without putting words in his mouth that were all wrong. "I came here because I—"

"Oh, please, give me a break. In December you couldn't get out of here fast enough. Obviously, marriage wasn't on your mind then. And if you would just be honest with yourself, you'd admit that it's only on your mind now because I'm pregnant.''

"There is no talking to you, is there?'' Jack muttered, so confounded by his inability to get through to her that he simply gave up.

"I told you in March that the time for talking had long passed. That is even truer now.''

"Only because you refuse to *listen* to me.''

Jack shoved a hand through his hair, barely resisting the urge to take her by the shoulders and give her a good shake. Or maybe kiss her so senseless she'd finally shut up long enough to hear what he was trying to say.

"I walked out on you in December because I was afraid of what getting involved with you would cost me emotionally. I thought if I lived a solitary life, I'd never again suffer the way I did when Cindy died. I'm still afraid. I won't deny it. But I'm willing to take the risk. I want to marry you, Abby, not out of a sense of duty, but because I truly care about you and about our child.''

"I wish I could believe you, Jack, but your reputation precedes you,'' Abby said, her voice sounding sad. "You're one of the good guys, and good guys always do the right thing, no matter what it costs them. It's not in your nature to get a girl pregnant then leave her to fend for herself. And I appreciate that—really, I do.

"But you don't need to have your life screwed up because of a mishap during one night of recreational sex. And you certainly don't have to pretend to care about me any more than you care about anyone else. I'm perfectly capable of fending for myself and my baby, and that's exactly what I plan to do.'' She hesitated a moment, then gestured toward the front door. "Now I think it would be best if you left."

Jack wanted to argue with her further, but considering her present frame of mind, he had to finally admit that nothing more he could say would do him any good. In fact, words alone weren't going to get him anywhere with her. The only way to prove to her that he cared about her was to *show* her. And that would take time—time he could only hope she would give him.

Walking away now wouldn't be easy, but it just might buy another opportunity to present his case. Abby's defenses had been up since she'd joined him in the living room, and they would stay up as long as he was there. But a few days from now, after she'd thought about all he'd said—as she surely would— maybe her attitude toward him would be less caustic.

"All right, if that's what you want," he agreed. "But only if you promise to see me again before you leave town. I'd like to try to work out some way that I can help provide for our child. I'm assuming you're not going to want me to be a part of his or her life, so that seems like the least I can do. I wouldn't want my child to grow up thinking that I'm some kind of deadbeat, especially when we both know that isn't true."

"I suppose that would be all right," Abby replied, somewhat grudgingly. "But I'm only going to be here three weeks. Then I'm going back to San Francisco. And I'm not going to change my mind about marrying you."

"I don't expect you to." He tucked his hands in the pockets of his shorts, paused a long moment, then spoke aloud the one thought he hadn't wanted to consider in the hope that she would somehow disprove it. "Not if you don't love me the way you said you did that night."

Abby's cheeks took on a bright red hue as her gaze slid away from his.

"We all say things we don't really mean at one time or another," she murmured, twisting her fingers together so tightly her knuckles turned white.

"My point exactly," Jack said, his spirits soaring. As he recalled, Abby had never been able to lie convincingly, and that still seemed to be the case. "I'll call you in a few days. Maybe then we can discuss our options in a calmer, more thoughtful manner."

"Yes, of course…in a few days," Abby acknowledged, refusing to meet his gaze again.

"Enjoy the flowers." Giving Abby a wide berth, Jack headed for the door to let himself out, the slightest of smiles tugging at the corner of his mouth.

"I will."

Finally out of Abby's sight, Jack allowed his smile to turn into a grin as he crossed to his car. She might have won this round, but he wasn't down and out yet.

With a blush and a shift of her eyes, she had given him the most powerful incentive of all to win her over. She loved him as he loved her, and somehow love would find a way.

Chapter Thirteen

"And then what did he do?" Judith asked as she set a plate of scrambled eggs, bacon and toast in front of Abby.

"He left," Abby replied as she dug into her breakfast.

After a restless night brought on as much by Jack's visit as by her overly long afternoon nap, Abby had crawled out of bed just after dawn, showered and dressed in khaki shorts with a comfortable elastic waist and a bright yellow T-shirt, and set off for her grandparents' apartment. She had known they would be up and about despite the early hour. She had also known her unexpected arrival would be as welcome as it had been.

She had needed to talk to someone about Jack's proposal—someone who would listen sympathetically, then offer sound advice, preferably supportive of the decision she had already made.

As Judith prepared breakfast, she and Hank had listened quietly while Abby related the events of the previous day. She told them about running into Jack at the real estate agency, how she inadvertently revealed her pregnancy, and his subsequent visit to her mother's house where he had asked her to marry him.

All that she had left out of her recitation was his mention of *her* feelings for *him*—feelings she had revealed that night in December and, until yesterday, had been fairly sure he'd failed to remember.

"Well, Abby, what I can't understand is why you're so bound and determined to run him off," Hank commented as he slathered strawberry jam on a slice of toast. "You must have had some fondness for each other the night you made that baby." He glanced at her, a twinkle in his eyes. "And he sounds like a decent fellow, willing to accept his responsibilities. These days, most men wouldn't bother. In my opinion, you could do a heck of a lot worse."

"But Jack Randall isn't in love with me," Abby said, keeping her tone matter-of-fact. "I knew that in December and I know it now. He only proposed because he considers it his duty. And as I've told Gran several times already, I don't want or need his charity."

"Talking about love can be hard for some men. Sometimes they're better at showing it," Judith pointed out, joining Abby and Hank at the table.

"When we were together in December, Jack told me how much he'd loved his wife," Abby admitted. "He didn't seem to have any trouble saying the word, then."

"But he hasn't said that he loves you?"

Feigning interest in forking up the last of her eggs, Abby looked away from her grandmother's questioning gaze and shook her head.

"What if he did?" Judith prodded. "Would you agree to marry him?"

If she thought that Jack really, truly loved her, she would marry him in a minute, Abby acknowledged, though she didn't say as much aloud. No sense allowing her grandparents to get their hopes up.

"Jack is not the type to say something he doesn't mean," she hedged instead. "He's concerned about my well-being and the baby's, but that's as far as his feelings for us go."

"Concern for another person, especially if that person is the mother of your child, can easily grow into love, Abby," her grandmother insisted. "I've seen it happen more often than not over the years."

"But there's no guarantee that it will," Abby countered, refusing to abandon her position. "And I'm not going to put myself in a situation where I have to be grateful for whatever crumbs of affection some man chooses to toss my way. I saw what that did to my mother. I'm not going to let the same thing happen to me."

"Larissa was a much different person than you are," Judith said. "She wanted fame and fortune more than anything, but she thought she could get it the easy way by marrying money. She made some unfortunate choices at a very young age, and when things didn't turn out quite the way she anticipated, she never could seem to pull herself together again.

"She never really talked about your father. All I know for sure is that he came from a wealthy family, and she must have loved him very much. I have a feeling he must have been married, too. I'm guessing that's why he abandoned her when she needed him most. He hurt her badly, no doubt about it. But she never let that color her feelings for you. She always loved you, in her own way.

"But she had a hard time being alone with herself when she came back to Promise, with you just a baby, only a few months old. She seemed to need to have a man around to fill the void, and yet, none of them really did her any lasting good."

"Because they didn't really love her and she knew it," Abby pointed out, putting into words what seemed so very obvious to her.

"Or because she felt too unworthy to ever really *let* any of them love her," Judith murmured, shooting a meaningful look Abby's way.

"Like I said, Gran, I'm not my mother. I don't *feel* unworthy of Jack Randall's love. I've simply accepted the fact that we don't share certain…emotions for each other, and we never will. He married the love of his life years ago. As for me, I guess I haven't met mine yet."

Looking away from her grandmother's piercing gaze so as not to give away the bald-faced lie she'd told, Abby stood and gathered their empty plates. From the corner of her eye, she saw her grandfather watching her, a smile playing around the corners of his mouth.

"What?" she asked when he put a hand on her arm.

"I was just thinking that you shouldn't protest quite so much. You might end up convincing yourself of something that isn't really true."

"Oh, Granddad..." Abby smiled and shook her head. "I'm just trying to be sensible, the way you and Gran have always taught me to be."

"Well, there's sensible, and then there's stubborn to the point of being downright pigheaded," Hank said.

"So, you think I'm being pigheaded, huh?"

"Not exactly. But you seem to be trying awfully hard to deny your true feelings. That's no way to live, either. Look what that did to your mother. Ever since the day she brought you home to us, something was eating her up inside, but she never would admit it. That, as much as anything, was what made her so restless, and in the end, so unhappy, too."

Aware that she had said all she could in her own defense, Abby opted to change the subject.

"Speaking of my mother," she began as she ran hot water into the sink to wash the dishes. "I was wondering if you two wanted to help me go through her things. I don't want to give away anything of hers that you'd like to have. And I don't want to take anything for myself that you'd like to have, either. We can have a garage sale after the house sells to dispose of the larger pieces of furniture we won't be keeping. But I'd like to box up her clothes and dishes—things like that—to donate to one of the local churches before I go back to San Francisco. Unless you'd rather I wait..."

"Oh, no, dear," Judith said. "That sounds like a good idea to me. Why don't you go through everything on your own and set aside what you'd like to keep? Then I'll take a look at whatever's left while we help you pack the boxes."

"I thought I'd tackle it one room at a time, starting with my bedroom."

"I'll see about getting some cardboard boxes for you," Hank offered.

"Thanks, Granddad. That would be a big help."

"Don't go doing any heavy lifting, now," Judith warned. "We can always hire somebody to give us a hand, if necessary."

"No climbing ladders, either," Hank added. "Just tell me when you're ready for me, and I'll stop by and empty the top shelves of the closets for you."

"I promise—no heavy lifting and no climbing ladders," Abby said, then mentioned the other, related, subject that had been on her mind for the past couple of months. "We should talk some more about your moving to San Francisco, too. Once the house sells, we won't have any real ties to Promise anymore, and living with me, you'd be able to watch your great-grandchild grow up. I want you to be a part of my baby's life on daily basis, not just the few times a year we would be able to visit if you stayed here."

"But this has always been our home, Abby," Judith reminded her. "And we don't ever want to be a burden to you, either."

"We can make a new home together in San Francisco, and you will never, *ever*, be a burden to me," Abby insisted.

"Well, we'll think about it. But we're not making any promises, are we, Hank?"

"Nope…no promises," Hank agreed.

"Fair enough."

Aware that she'd made her case as best she could, Abby rinsed the last dish, then dried her hands on a towel. A glance at the clock on the wall told her

she'd better hurry or she would be late for her scheduled meeting with Jan Nelson.

"I'd better get back to the house," she said. "I'm
supposed to meet with the real estate agent at eight-
thirty so she can have a look at the place and take
some photos to run with the ad she's going to put in
the paper."

"We're going to bingo at St. Edward's tonight.
Starts at six-thirty. We usually stop at the cafeteria
in the mall for an early dinner first. You're welcome
to go with us," Judith invited.

"I think I'll pass," Abby replied, giving her
grandmother a kiss on the cheek. "But if you're free
tomorrow night, why don't you come over for dinner? I'm making pot roast, with or without you."

"Pot roast, you say? We'll be there," Hank answered, giving her a hug.

"Yes, we most certainly will," Judith seconded.

Abby made it back to her mother's house with
more than enough time to spare before Jan Nelson
arrived. The agent walked through the house with
her, murmuring her approval. To Abby's relief, no
major repairs seemed to be needed, although Jan did
warn that an inspector might come across something
during a more thorough examination of the premises.
In the meantime, however, she advised Abby not to
worry.

After taking pictures of the outside of the house,
front and back, Jan sped off to her next appointment,
leaving Abby with the promise that she would be in
touch. As she watched the agent pull out of the driveway, Abby was grateful that she didn't have a moment more to spare.

In the short time they'd been together, Jan had

managed to slip in several comments about Jack, each one more pointed than the last, and each obviously meant to lead Abby into sharing confidences, woman to woman. Abby had replied in monosyllables, being as vague as she could. Given more time, however, Jan would have eventually broken her down.

She couldn't blame the woman for being curious, considering the way Jack had behaved at the agency. But Abby wasn't about to share the details of her relationship, such as it was, with Promise's most eligible bachelor, with a woman she hardly knew.

On her own at last, Abby took advantage of the burst of energy she'd no doubt gotten from the hearty breakfast she'd eaten. She went straight to her bedroom and busied herself emptying the dresser drawers and the closet, including the shelves which she was just tall enough to reach by standing on her toes.

Most of what she'd left there in the way of clothing wasn't any use to her now, but everything was still in good enough shape to donate to those less fortunate. As she sorted and folded shirts and shorts, T-shirts and jeans, she thought about the conversation she'd had with her grandparents.

Not so much what they'd said about Jack. They were determined to think the best of him, and Abby saw no reason to disillusion them. Her mind was made up where he was concerned, and she wasn't going to be swayed by their lobbying on his behalf.

Instead, Abby thought of what her grandparents had said about her father and Larissa. They had told her more about them, and the relationship they'd had, than they ever had before, and in doing so, had shed new light on why her mother had always seemed so unhappy.

Larissa had obviously loved Abby's father enough to bear his child, yet she had never told her anything about him. Abby didn't even know his name, and she was fairly sure her grandparents didn't, either.

Larissa had met him in Las Vegas, but how long they'd known each other before she'd gotten pregnant was anybody's guess. All that Abby knew for certain was that they'd never married, and by the time she was born Larissa had been on her own again. Abby had always assumed he'd died a tragic death, though she couldn't say why. And she'd always wondered if he, or anyone in his family, had known about her existence.

Each time she had tried to ask Larissa about him, her mother had cut her off almost angrily, insisting that there were some things Abby was better off not knowing, not only about her father, but about Larissa, too. Still, Abby had been curious, and as she'd grown older, she had pressed her mother for more and more information.

During what had turned out to be their final showdown on the subject when Abby was in high school, Larissa had ended up locking herself in her bedroom where she'd sobbed hysterically for almost an hour. So frightened had Abby been by her mother's behavior, she'd vowed never to bring up the subject again, and she'd been as good as her word in all the years since.

Now, pregnant with her own child, she wished she had made more of an effort to talk to Larissa about her father once she'd reached adulthood. Surely in recent years, her mother would have mellowed somewhat on the subject.

There were things an expectant mother was expected to know about her family's medical history that would forever be a mystery to her. Luckily, she had always been healthy herself, as had her mother and her grandparents. She could only hope the same was true of her father's family.

Her father's family…and hers, as well, Abby thought as she sat amid the piles of old clothes on her bed. Somewhere out there, she could very well have a whole slew of blood relatives she'd never met.

Did they know about her, or had her existence never been revealed? What if her father had been married, as Gran had surmised? What if she had brothers and sisters, another set of grandparents, aunts and uncles and cousins?

Abby wanted to find out, and yet, she didn't. What if she managed to track down her father's family, impossible task that it seemed, and they wanted nothing to do with her? Or, just as problematic, what if *she* wanted nothing to do with *them?* There was no guarantee her father's family would be the kind of family she'd want to acknowledge. Especially if they had known about her and Larissa all these years, and had done nothing to acknowledge *them.*

Abby had always envied her friends who had more traditional families, and she'd felt that her friends who'd had sisters had been doubly blessed. No matter how they had battled, they had always had a special closeness that had left Abby feeling more alone than seemed natural.

But she had her baby, now, she reminded herself, heading to the kitchen for a glass of juice. And she

still had Hank and Judith. They were her family—
all the family she needed. No sense feeling sad about
what she didn't have when she had more than enough
to be grateful for already.

There was Jack's desire to be a part of their child's
life, as well, she also acknowledged as she stood by
the counter and sipped the tangy apple juice she'd
poured. Her baby would know his or her father and,
she was sure, benefit from it.

She would have to set certain boundaries, of
course, and Jack would have requirements of his
own. But within whatever limits they agreed upon,
she knew he would do his best to be a good father.

Her child would never have to ask the kind of
questions Abby had just been asking herself. Her
child would grow up secure in the knowledge that
he or she was loved by both parents despite the fact
that they didn't love each other.

Or, perhaps more truthfully, despite the fact that
one of them didn't love the other.

Chapter Fourteen

For two days following his unfortunately-put proposal to Abby, Jack schooled himself to be patient. He had made yet another mistake where she was concerned, taking for granted that wooing her wouldn't be necessary under the circumstances.

He had assumed that saying he wanted to marry her was the same as saying he loved her. Why else, in this day and age, would any man offer to make such a commitment? He hadn't taken into account the awful note he had left for her in December, and how she insisted on interpreting it, even after he'd disavowed the cruel words he'd written.

No matter how he had tried, he hadn't been able to convince her that he'd been anything but honest with her then. Because, of course, he *had* been, in a muddled, fearful sort of way.

But he had been equally honest with her Tuesday

night, and he'd been thinking clearly, then. Surely she had seen the difference between a note hastily scribbled in a moment of pure, unadulterated panic and words spoken from the heart, face-to-face.

Instead, she seemed to have gotten it into her head that he was only doing what he considered his duty, and attempting to convince her otherwise with words alone had proved to be impossible. Abby had made it clear that she wanted nothing more to do with him.

Quick thinking on his part had gained him another opportunity to show her how he felt. But he didn't want to risk coming on too strong or too fast. She might just shut him out completely.

First and foremost, he had to regain her trust. Then he had to convince her that not only was his love for her real, but he was also worthy of *her* love in return. All within the few weeks she'd said she would be in Promise.

Just thinking about the task he had ahead of him was enough to make Jack want to weep. But there was too much at stake to wimp out now. A future without Abby was one he refused to contemplate.

They had been meant to be together that night in December, and they were meant to be together ever after. He hadn't wanted to believe it then, but now he did. And he was determined to find a way to make Abby a believer, too—regardless of what it cost him.

There was one chink in her armor that kept him from the brink of utter despair, and he reminded himself of it regularly as the days passed. In December, Abby had said that she loved him as she'd curled close to him in her bed. And when he'd called her on it Tuesday night, she hadn't been able to deny it.

Her hedging had signalled an inner conflict he had every intention of using to his advantage.

Jack had decided that giving Abby a couple of days to think about what he'd said, and what she'd said, would be the best way to proceed. No matter how she tried to harden her heart, she would have to acknowledge his sincerity and concern. And she obviously couldn't set aside her feelings for him.

Since both factors worked in his favor, surely she would be more open to his next overture. Once he decided on one that wouldn't have her slamming the door in his face.

Since he had left her mother's house on Tuesday evening, Jack had caught several glimpses of Abby around town. That he'd put himself in places where he had hoped she would be hadn't hurt. Bumping into someone in a small town wasn't that hard, after all.

Abby hadn't seemed to notice him, though. And Jack had resisted calling attention to himself, mostly because all he'd really wanted to do was whisk her away to someplace private and try to make things right between them.

Fortunately, he'd had sense enough to know that all the use of caveman tactics would likely gain him was a restraining order. But the alternative—calm, quiet discussion of thoughts and feelings—didn't seem like the way to get him what he wanted, either.

There had to be a happy medium between words and actions—one that would neither bore Abby half to death nor scare her witless. But so far, he hadn't made much progress figuring out exactly what that happy medium might entail.

To keep from driving himself crazy, Jack had tried

to focus on his work, putting in extra hours at the clinic as he was doing that Friday morning. He wasn't scheduled to start seeing his own patients until noon, but he had come in several hours early to help Aaron Post with walk-ins and minor emergencies.

He had just finished stitching a nasty cut on a construction worker's forearm, and was on his way to the reception desk to see if there was anyone else awaiting medical attention, when he heard the vaguely familiar voice of a woman speaking in a confidential tone to the clinic's receptionist, Edna Howell.

"Surely, you remember her mother—Larissa Summers? Always up to no good, an embarrassment to poor Hank and Judith..."

"Oh, yes, I remember Larissa. We had some classes together at Promise High School. She *was* a wild one," Mrs. Howell replied. "Came to a tragic end just after Christmas, didn't she, Constance?"

At the receptionist's mention of the other woman's name, Jack paused just out of sight, a frown furrowing his forehead. So, it was Abby's neighbor out in the clinic's waiting room, busy spreading gossip. He could just imagine what was coming next, and Constance Beckworth didn't disappoint him.

"Yes, she did, and now her daughter's back in town, supposedly to sell the house. But I think she's trying to get her hooks into Dr. Randall. I saw them together in December, then again Tuesday night. And she's pregnant, you know—about four or five months from what I can determine. No doubt she's claiming the brat is his, but a girl like that, with

a mother like Larissa…that baby could be anybody's.''

As Jack listened to what Constance Beckworth
was saying, his anger at the woman boiled up, very
nearly getting the better of him. Not because she was
talking about him, but because she was talking about
Abby, and in such an unconscionably derogatory
manner that she deserved a good throttling. One he
would have dearly liked to give her.

He had tried to make allowances for the woman,
giving her the benefit of the doubt the few times he'd
seen her nosing around in Abby business. But she
had gone much too far, telling tales about the woman
he loved to one of his own employees.

How dare Constance Beckworth insinuate that
Abby was a liar and a cheat, out to trick him for her
own benefit when that was the furthest thing from
the truth?

''What's that old saying about the apple not falling
far from the tree?'' Mrs. Howell asked, her tone taking on a smug, sly note that made Jack realize she
was not only eating up every word the Beckworth
woman had to say, but also planning on repeating all
she'd heard to anyone willing to listen.

As far as Jack could see, there was only one way
to silence the two of them, and protect Abby into the
bargain. Stepping into view, he eyed first Mrs. Beckworth, then Mrs. Howell, while he also noted with
relief that the waiting room was otherwise empty.

Though he leveled a stern gaze their way, he tried
to keep his overall expression bland. And when he
spoke, he was surprised at how mild his voice
sounded, considering how his emotions roiled.

''I couldn't help but overhear your conversation,''

he began, taking pleasure in the bright red flush that suffused Edna Howell's usually pale face.

Good—she *should* be embarrassed. Constance Beckworth, however, looked more miffed than anything. As if he had some nerve eavesdropping on *her* conversation, then taking exception to it.

"Oh, Dr. Randall, we didn't mean any harm," Mrs. Howell said, not quite meeting his gaze.

"I'm glad to hear that because you were talking about my fiancée—a woman I not only love very much, but also look forward to spending the rest of my life with."

The words came out of his mouth before he had a chance to even consider the Pandora's box he was opening for Abby as well as himself. She had *not* agreed to marry him, and if she found out from anyone but him that he was telling people she had, she was going to be furious.

At that moment, though, all he wanted to do was protect her from the kind of harmful, hurtful, *hateful* gossip Constance Beckworth seemed determined to spread. And the best way to do that, at least in his opinion, was to draw Abby under the protective mantle the Randall name could provide in small-town Promise, Nevada.

Even Constance Beckworth would think twice before she slandered the Randall family, of which he had just indicated Abby Summers would very soon be a part.

"Oh, really?" Mrs. Beckworth eyed him disbelievingly. "Rather sudden, your…engagement, isn't it?"

"Not at all. We've been making wedding plans for several months, but Abby wasn't able to get back to Promise until now. We'll be making our official announcement next week.''

"Your parents must be…delighted.'' The woman all but sneered.

"Of course, they are. Abby's a wonderful woman. They love her as much as I do.''

Jack tried not to think of how deeply he was digging himself in, or of how righteously angry Abby was going to be when he told her what he'd done. He just kept embellishing his original lie while at the same time assuring himself that his intentions were good.

Surely that would count for something down the line.

"I'm so happy to hear that,'' Constance muttered, the malicious look in her rheumy old eyes belying her words.

"Were you waiting to see a doctor?'' Jack asked, turning businesslike to end any further musings on Mrs. Beckworth's part.

"Dr. Post has seen me already. I was just on my way out, thank you.''

"Well, don't let us keep you any longer. I'm sure you have a full day ahead of you.'' Jack smiled as he walked to the clinic door and opened it for her with a gallant flourish.

"Quite full,'' Mrs. Beckworth assured him as she sailed out the door, her head held regally high.

Glad to see the back of her, Jack closed the door, then fixed his gaze on Edna Howell.

"I'm sorry, Dr. Randall. I had no business—'' she began, looking away self-consciously.

"None at all,'' Jack cut in sternly. "And if I hear of anything similar happening here again, you'll be out the door so fast your head will spin. Understood?''

"Yes, Doctor."

"I'll be in my office if anyone needs me."

Turning on his heel, Jack strode down the hallway and into his office. He shut the door firmly, crossed to his desk and sank into his chair.

He couldn't quite believe what he'd done. But that didn't make the neat little corner he'd talked himself into any less inescapable.

He was going to have to tell Abby about their engagement, and he was going to have to do it just as soon as he finished seeing his scheduled patients late that afternoon. Then he might just be able to mollify her enough to go along with him as he hadn't a hope of doing if she heard about it from anyone else.

He was going to have to convince her that pretending they were engaged would be to her benefit— as it would be. Or, at the very least, to her grandparents' benefit. She wouldn't want *them* hurt by rude gossip even if she didn't care about it herself.

And then, he might just be able to make their *engagement* work to *his* benefit, as well, he realized, his spirits rising.

What better way to court Abby than as her fiancé, even *pretend* fiancé? There were certain rituals they would be expected to follow, and in doing so, they would be forced to spend time together. Time when he would finally have a chance to convince her there was nothing at all *pretend* about his feelings for her.

Constance Beckworth would probably have a fit if she ever discovered what a good deed she'd done that morning. Of course, being a doctor, and ever-caring of others' well-being, Jack would never tell her.

But it gave him great pleasure to know the old woman's unkind intentions just might have another effect altogether on Abby Summers' life, and on his, as well.

Smiling to himself, Jack reached for the telephone and dialed Abby's telephone number, then warned himself not to start feeling too cocky. Abby would more than likely fight him all the way about embarking on a *pretend* engagement. But he had sound reasoning on his side, and he wasn't averse to using it on her to get what he wanted.

To Jack's relief, Abby answered the phone after a couple of rings.

"Hey, Abby, it's Jack Randall," he began. "I was wondering if I could stop by to see you this evening, say about six o'clock. I'll bring dinner...."

Chapter Fifteen

Abby went out of her way to make sure she was wide awake and neatly dressed in a sleeveless, collared, loose-fitting emerald-green knit dress and flat, strappy sandals half an hour before Jack's appointed time of arrival Friday evening.

When he had called that morning to ask if she would be free around six o'clock, she had wanted to put him off. But he had sounded so eager to see her, and that, in turn, had helped to boost her flagging spirits.

He had also promised to bring dinner—a fully loaded pizza from the Brick Oven Pizzeria—something she'd been craving since she'd been back in town, but hadn't dared order because she wouldn't have been able to stop herself from eating the whole pie alone.

And, of course, there was the little matter of how

much responsibility for their child he wanted to assume. The sooner they could come to some agreement, the better for all concerned.

Abby didn't want to cut Jack out of their child's life completely. But neither did she want him to think he could dictate to her in any way regarding what he considered the baby's best interests.

She was fully prepared to take on the duties of a single, working mother, and she was just as capable as he of providing for the baby financially. She wasn't about to take anything from him that would make her beholden to him. He was more than welcome to be a part of their child's life, but he would have to understand that she wasn't going to let him run *her* life into the bargain.

All of which Abby repeated to herself as she set out plates, silverware, glasses and napkins on the kitchen table in preparation for Jack's arrival.

As good as his word, he rang the doorbell at six o'clock sharp, a huge, steaming Brick Oven box in hand. As Abby opened the door to him, it was all she could do to keep from snatching the box away from him and grabbing a slice of the pizza right there in the entryway.

"Smells wonderful," she said, choosing not to demur in any way. "I have plates ready in the kitchen."

"Good thing," Jack replied, following her lead through the living room. "It was hard enough waiting to sample a slice on the drive over here. I don't think I could pretend not to be hungry for even five minutes more."

While Abby took a beer from the refrigerator for Jack and refilled her glass of raspberry iced tea, he set the box on the table and opened the lid. Abby thought she would swoon in ecstasy as the smoky aroma of hand-tossed crust, spicy sauce, gooey cheeses, Italian sausage and a medley of fresh vegetables intensified to fill the kitchen.

She was so glad she wasn't sick all the time the way some women were during pregnancy. She had suffered several bouts of morning sickness the first couple of months, but since then, her appetite had been rather hearty—to say the least.

She would probably be sorry after the baby was born and she had a lot of weight to lose. Until then, however, she planned to heed her body's cravings as healthfully as she could so her baby would get all the nourishment possible. And the pizza Jack had brought for dinner *did* include something from most, if not all, the basic food groups.

They ate in companionable silence for several minutes, murmuring about how the Brick Oven's pizzas were just as good as they had been twelve years ago, and wasn't it great that some things hadn't changed. Once their initial hunger had been somewhat sated, Jack asked Abby how she had been feeling for the past few days and what she'd been up to since he'd last seen her.

Abby assured him that she was feeling just fine, then went on to tell him about the progress, little as it was, that she had made cleaning out the various nooks and crannies in her mother's house.

"I haven't gotten nearly as much done as I thought I would," she admitted with a rueful shake of her head. "Either I get sidetracked, looking through old yearbooks or writing names and dates on the backs of photographs, or I just *have* to take a nap. I'm only going to be here a couple more weeks, and I wanted to finish sorting through everything at least once.'' Pausing, Abby lifted her third—and last, she silently swore—large slice of pizza from the box, then added, ''Jan Nelson stopped by Wednesday morning to take some photographs. She said the house looked like it was in really good shape. I don't have to worry about painting or wallpapering or replacing the carpet to get the asking price.

''Apparently, the town has become popular among retirees looking for a place close enough to Las Vegas for a day trip without the big city hassle. Some former residents have also been returning because of the quality of life here. Jan mentioned, too, that a small computer software company had recently relocated to Promise because of the comparatively favorable cost of living, and several other companies are considering a similar move.''

''Who would have thought our little town would one day be so desirable?'' Jack asked. ''We couldn't get out of here fast enough, could we?''

''I know I couldn't,'' Abby admitted. ''But you've come back, and from the way Jan talked, it sounds like you're planning to stay. She said you made an offer on a house and several acres of land just north of town. In fact, she seemed to think I already knew all about it, probably because of the way you ambushed me at the agency Tuesday afternoon.''

''It's the old Domar place,'' Jack said by way of explanation, obviously choosing to ignore her last remark as he stood and crossed to the refrigerator. ''Mind if I have another beer?''

''Not at all. I bought them for you.''

''Thanks.'' Jack helped himself to a beer, then returned to the table where he eyed the two remaining slices of pizza with seeming indecision.

"Go ahead," Abby urged, pushing the box toward him with a slight smile. Not to be sidetracked, she then prodded gently, "The Domar place?"

"Yeah, the Domar place. It needs a lot of work, mostly cosmetic, but I've got the time to paint and hang wallpaper. And the location is really nice—I have neighbors just down the road on either side, yet it's still pretty quiet. There's a small orchard behind the house with a little creek cutting through it, too."

"Sounds lovely," Abby said. "And thanks for enlightening me. I won't feel quite so dumb the next time I see Jan and she mentions it, as I'm sure she will."

"Listen, Abby, I'm really sorry for coming on to you the way I did Tuesday afternoon." Jack shifted in his chair, not quite meeting her gaze. "I should have known better than to do something like that, especially in front of Jan. Not that she's mean-spirited. She's pretty good at putting two and two together, though, and in her line of work, she's out talking to everybody. And around here, it takes very little to start the rumor mill grinding," he added, nervously running a finger along the side of his glass.

"Very little, indeed." Abby hesitated a moment, then reached out to touch Jack's arm. "I hope your good name isn't being slandered because we were seen together at the real estate agency," she said, only half-teasingly.

"I wouldn't care if it was." He took her hand in his and squeezed her fingers gently. "In fact, I'd be proud to have my name linked with yours. Surely you haven't forgotten that I've asked you to marry me.''

"And I've said no," Abby reminded him, trying, unsuccessfully, to free her hand from his hold.

"I wish you would reconsider—"

"Oh, Jack, you know I can't," she cut in, hating to have to replay this particular discussion again.

It had been hard enough to be firm about her refusal to marry him the first time around. Now, sitting here with him so companionably, she'd had a taste of what it would be like to have him in her life on a permanent basis, sharing a meal and good conversation, and her defenses were decidedly down.

"Because I've had to tell some people that we're engaged," he plowed ahead, ignoring her protest.

Abby stared at him speechlessly for several seconds as she tried to wrap her mind around what he'd just said.

"You had to do *what?*" she demanded at last, sure that she had heard him wrong.

"I had to tell some people we're engaged," he repeated as calmly as if he were relaying the time of day.

"And *why* would you have to do *that,* Jack Randall? Especially when it is not, and never will be, *true.*" Angrily, she snatched her hand free, pushed away from the table and strode to the sink, then rounded on him, her hands braced on her hips, waiting for him to reply.

"Your neighbor, Constance Beckworth, was at the clinic this morning. I overheard her talking to Edna Howell, our receptionist. She was saying all sorts of unfair, untrue, totally nasty-minded things about you—Mrs. Beckworth, that is. And, well…I just… lost it.

"I walked in on the two of them, told them they were talking about my fiancée and I didn't appreciate it. They were both embarrassed, as they should have been. But now, they're going to be spreading another kind of rumor around town. One that's much more complimentary, of course. At least to my way of thinking," he finished, eyeing her apologetically.

"But *not* true," Abby repeated, trying to hold on to her anger when she wasn't sure if what she really wanted to do was laugh or cry.

She knew exactly what Jack had done. He had come to her defense, just as he had twelve years ago, using his good name to shield her. He had been thinking of her, first and foremost, of that Abby had no doubt. And because he'd obviously meant well, she couldn't really be all that upset with him.

But she no longer needed his protection. She was an intelligent, educated woman to whom a bit of small-town gossip meant nothing.

Well, all right, it *did* hurt to know that her mother's neighbor thought poorly of her. But not enough to fabricate a lie as Jack had done—albeit out of *his* hurt for her.

"It could be true," he said, an unmistakably hopeful gleam in his eyes as he stood, too. "At least for the rest of the time you're in Promise."

"Oh, no—" Abby protested, not only afraid of where he was headed, but also of how easily she could be tempted to follow—for *his* sake rather than her own.

Because he had been thinking about her, and *protecting* her in the only way he'd known how.

"We could just pretend to be engaged for the next couple of weeks," he went on, as if she hadn't spoken. "That way, all the old biddies won't have anything but good to say about us."

"They've never had anything but good to say about *you,* Jack Randall, and you know it," Abby retorted. "And I really don't care what anybody says about me. I'm a big girl now. Sticks and stones, and all that…" Shrugging, she crossed her arms over her chest.

He wasn't going to talk her into such foolishness. He *wasn't*—

"But I care. You're the mother of my child, and the woman I want to marry."

"Don't go there, Jack," she cautioned, shooting him a warning glare.

"All right, I won't. But you *are* carrying my child, and I won't have anybody saying anything hurtful about you if I can help it. And the best way to prevent that from happening is to pretend we're engaged," he finished in a maddeningly reasonable tone of voice.

"What happens when I leave town—and I *am* leaving—in a couple of weeks?" Abby asked, beginning to weaken and hating herself for it. She couldn't disallow Jack's feelings completely. But a *pretend* engagement could prove to be more entangling than he was willing to foresee. "What are you going to say to people—people like your parents—then?"

"I'll say that our breakup was my fault. That I gave you good reason to change your mind about marrying me," Jack assured her without batting an eye.

"What good reason?"

"I'll think of something, and I won't put you in a bad light, either. I swear."

"I'm not going to let my grandparents get their hopes up. I'm going to make sure they know from the start that we're not really getting married."

"That's fine with me."

Aware of the faintest edge of triumph lurking in the tenderness of Jack's smile, Abby looked away. Much as she wanted to tell him what he could do with his idea, and it wasn't something pleasant, she couldn't seem to get the words out. She had put up a good fight, but in the end, she couldn't be totally selfish.

In his own good, kind and decent way, Jack had been thinking of her and their baby. To reject him completely would make a liar out of him in front of the whole town, and he deserved better than that.

What would it hurt to go along with him for the few remaining weeks she'd be in Promise, especially as long as her grandparents knew the truth? Once she left town, he could make whatever excuses he wanted as long as he didn't cause Hank and Judith any grief. She would be home again in San Francisco, with the weeks she'd spent in Promise, Nevada no more than an unfortunate memory.

"All right," she agreed at last. "I'll go along with you on this as long as you understand that our engagement is just pretend, and that in two weeks I'm going back to the life I've made for myself in San Francisco."

"I understand completely," he assured her in a solemn tone of voice, though his eyes twinkled in a way that gave her pause. "I imagine you'll want to talk to your grandparents first thing in the morning. I'll tell my parents tomorrow, too. They'll want to meet you, of course. How about tomorrow night? I'll make all the arrangements. I'd like to meet your grandparents, too. Why don't we take them to brunch at the café on Sunday? And we'll have to put an announcement in the local paper, too...."

Listening to Jack launch into his plans, Abby experienced the tiniest shiver of disquiet. They were just pretending to be engaged. Really, they *were*. She would do well not only to remember it herself, but also to remind Jack of it as often as possible.

She wasn't about to let the situation get out of hand. And she certainly wasn't going to start hoping and dreaming for the impossible. Jack Randall wasn't in love with her. He never had been, and he never would be. He was just being kind for the baby's sake, and only for the next two weeks.

And she didn't dare let herself forget it, even for a minute.

Chapter Sixteen

As he drove to Abby's mother's house on Saturday evening, Jack still couldn't quite believe that he had managed to talk Abby into agreeing to a pretend engagement. She had put up a good fight the night before—he had to give her credit for that. But in the end, she hadn't been able to make a liar out of him, even though she'd had every right to.

Obviously, she hadn't hardened her heart to him completely. But Jack reminded himself yet again not to start feeling cocky. He didn't dare take for granted the good luck he'd had so far because he knew he had a very thin line to walk in the days ahead.

Since Abby seemed bound and determined not to allow their engagement to turn into the real thing, he couldn't risk scaring her off by coming on too strong, too fast. If she scampered back to San Francisco sooner than she'd planned because he said or did something, even inadvertently, to make her feel pressured, he would find himself back at square one.

But neither could he allow Abby to think, even for a moment, that there was anything pretend about his feelings for her.

She didn't seem to have any trouble accepting the idea that he was too kind and decent to allow her to be hurt by idle gossip. Yet she stubbornly refused to consider the possibility that he loved her as truly, deeply and completely as any man could ever love a woman.

Only by *showing* her how much he cared for her, in every little way he could in the days ahead, would he have any chance of winning her over.

Jack hadn't wasted any time mapping out his campaign. Before he had left Abby on Friday night, he'd gotten her to agree, albeit reluctantly, to meet his parents Saturday evening. He had promised they would have a quiet dinner together, just the four of them. Unless Abby wanted to include her grandparents, which she hadn't.

She would go through the formality of introducing Jack to them at brunch on Sunday, if he insisted, as he had. Though she hadn't thought it was necessary since they would, according to her, know the whole truth, start to finish.

Jack had every intention of winning over Hank and Judith Summers the following day. Tonight, however, he would devote to winning over Abby, if only just the tiniest bit.

Pulling into the driveway of Abby's mother's house, he was relieved to see that Constance Beckworth wasn't outside. He didn't want his good mood spoiled, even temporarily, by her caustic comments.

Once she saw the announcement he'd sent to the *Promise Daily News* for the paper's Wednesday edition, and she received her invitation to Thursday night's cocktail party that his parents were hosting at the country club in his and Abby's honor, she should have mellowed enough toward Abby to end her gossiping. In the meantime, Jack would just as soon not have to speak to the woman.

Abby had obviously been waiting for his arrival. She opened the door as soon as he rang the bell, dressed in the same pretty yellow dress she'd been wearing when he had first seen her at the real estate agency. She had coiled her hair in an elegant twist, but a few errant strands curled around her face, easing the style's severity. She wore pearl-and-gold-bead earrings and a matching pearl-and-gold-bead choker that enhanced her creamy complexion.

She looked lovelier than ever to Jack. So lovely, in fact, that he wanted to scoop her into his arms, carry her into the house, kick the door shut, and completely forget about having dinner with his parents. But the way she clutched her purse in her white-knuckled fingers as she eyed him, grim-faced, put such a foolhardy notion immediately out of his mind.

''I'm ready,'' she announced, tipping her chin up as if she were about to be escorted to the guillotine.

''We're not actually expected for another hour,'' Jack admitted with a sheepish smile.

''But you said you would pick me up at six-thirty. I assumed we were going to go straight to your parents' house.'' Standing her ground in the doorway, Abby frowned at him disapprovingly.

''I thought we could have a drink first. Relax a little together before we join my parents.''

There was something else he planned to do before they went on to his parents' house, but he didn't want to tell her what it was while she could slam the door in his face. She already looked wound up enough.

"Well, all right." Grudgingly, she stepped back and let him into the house.

"Did you talk to your grandparents this morning?" he asked as he followed her into the living room and sat on the sofa.

"Yes."

Abby remained standing, her frown deepening as she lowered her gaze and fiddled with the clasp of her purse.

"How did they react to the news of our engagement?"

"They were thrilled," Abby said, still refusing to look at him. "Neither one of them seemed to believe for a minute that we were only pretending to protect my good name, no matter what I said." She hesitated, then glanced at him. "Maybe this isn't such a good idea, after all. They're just going to end up being hurt—"

"Not necessarily," Jack hastened to assure her. Though he couldn't say as much to Abby, he was pleased by her grandparents' positive reaction. "You're being honest with them, and who knows how things will turn out two weeks from now."

"*I* know," she shot back, meeting his gaze squarely. "What about your parents? What did they say when you told them you were not only engaged, but had a baby on the way?"

"They were thrilled, too," Jack said, quite honestly. "They're very anxious to meet you. My father's grilling some of his Alaskan salmon just for you, and my mother's baking her top secret cinnamon chocolate cake. When I left there, she was looking for the recipe so she could write out a copy for you. That, alone, means she already considers you a welcome addition to the family."

"Oh, Jack..." Abby sighed as she set her purse on the coffee table, then sank down next to him on the sofa. "I don't think I can go through with a pretend engagement, after all."

"Of course you can." He put an arm around her shoulders and gave her a hug. "It's only for a couple of weeks, and no one will think the worse of you if we break it off. I'll make sure of it."

"Not if, *when.* My decision is already made," she reminded him, stiffening her shoulders. "Now, about that drink you mentioned—what would you like to have? There's still some beer in the refrigerator."

When she started to get up, Jack caught her by the hand.

"I'm not really thirsty right now."

"But you said you came early—"

"Actually, I wanted to give you something before we go over to my parents' house," he cut in.

Standing, he dug in his pants pocket and pulled out a small, black velvet box as Abby eyed him skeptically.

"Jack, *no,*" she began, her gaze locking on the box.

Not giving her a chance to say more, he knelt in front of her, offered her his most charming grin, and flipped open the lid of the box with his thumb.

"Marry me, Abby Summers. Marry me, please."

She stared at the diamond ring nestled in the box

in utter consternation as a blush tinted her cheeks a bright pink.

"Don't be silly," she said breathlessly after a few moments. "We're only *pretending* to be engaged, and that certainly doesn't look like a *pretend* ring to me."

"It's not," he said, taking the two-carat, emerald-cut diamond ring with square-cut baguette diamonds on either side from the box.

"I can't accept it," she murmured, curling the fingers of her left hand into a fist. "I...I *can't.*"

"No one will believe we're engaged unless you do," Jack pointed out pragmatically. "Of course, if you don't like this particular ring, we can go to the jewelers on Monday and you can choose another one."

"I like it...very much," Abby conceded. "But it's...it's too big and too beautiful for just pretend."

"Not really, as long as you like it."

Allowing himself only the slightest smile, Jack took Abby's left hand in his and eased the glittering ring onto the appropriate finger.

The ring fit perfectly, and as he'd hoped, it looked as if it had been made for her slender, elegant hand.

"Lovely," he murmured. Lifting her hand to his lips, he pressed a gentle kiss to the back of her wrist, then released her. As he stood again, he checked his watch. "Well, we'd better go. We don't want to be late when there's Alaskan salmon and cinnamon chocolate cake on the menu, do we?"

Abby gazed up at him, a dazed look in her eyes that gave Jack's spirits another much needed lift. He had gambled on getting just such a response from her when he'd bought the ring that morning. She could have just as easily thrown him out on his ear.

But she was off-balance now—no longer quite so sure where the line between fantasy and reality fell. And that was exactly where he wanted her.

Once he got her to start feeling, even for a few moments at a time, that they were a couple, it wouldn't take that much more to actually make it so.

He considered the ring a first step in that direction. As long as it stayed on her finger, where she could see it and *feel* it every day, he would be on her mind, as well.

She would begin to realize, little by little, that some things, like his love for her, couldn't be feigned. Some things, like his love for her, were as real and lasting and true as the diamond he'd given her.

Abby sat on the sofa a few seconds longer, staring at the ring on her finger. Then, with an apparent mental shake, she grabbed her purse and stood, too, her expression once again pensive.

"What's wrong?" Jack asked as they started toward the door.

"Just a little nervous about meeting your parents," Abby answered.

"They're going to love you as much as I do," he said, his tone lighthearted.

"If you say so." Sounding unconvinced as they stepped outside, she turned to lock the door.

"You said I was one of the good guys, remember?" he prodded, taking her by the arm as they walked to his car.

Glancing up at him, she nodded wordlessly.

"Well, you don't think I'd have ended up that way if I'd been raised by jackals, do you?"

"No," she admitted with the first real smile he'd seen on her face that evening.

"Then relax, be yourself, and enjoy the evening, okay?"

"Okay."

Pausing at the car, with the door open, Jack bent and kissed Abby gently on the cheek.

"Trust me, everything is going to be all right."

"If you say so," she repeated, this time sounding as if she actually believed him.

Chapter Seventeen

Abby had never in her life been involved in such a whirlwind of social activity as she had since the night Jack suggested that they embark on a *pretend* engagement.

Saturday evening she and Jack had joined his parents for dinner at their lovely home in Promise's most exclusive neighborhood. Abby had dreaded meeting Elaine and J. B. Randall from the moment he suggested it, but there had been no way to avoid it sometime during the remaining two weeks she would be in Promise. They were the type of people who would want to get to know their only son's fiancée, and the sooner, the better.

Abby had spent most of that Saturday bracing herself for the likely possibility that Jack's parents would welcome her into the family with less-than-open arms. She had told herself it wouldn't matter since she and Jack weren't really getting married. But still, the prospect of spending several hours trying to make polite conversation with two people who probably wanted someone better for their son had held absolutely no appeal.

That the evening had turned out to be entirely different than Abby had anticipated had been a truly delightful surprise. So delightful, in fact, that she had found herself secretly wishing that she and Jack weren't just pretending, after all.

First Jack had given her the most beautiful diamond engagement ring she'd ever seen, and he'd done so in a manner that would have had her believing he really did love her enough to marry her—if she hadn't already known better.

For heaven's sake, he had gotten down on one knee, and though there had been a teasing glint in his eyes, his "marry me, please" had been spoken with such a ring of sincerity that she'd had to bite her lip to keep from saying "yes, yes, *yes,*" in reply.

With Jack's ring on her finger, Abby had been just off-balance enough that she hadn't had time to think about being nervous on the short drive to his parents' house. And once there, Jack's mother and father had drawn her into the Randall family circle with such warmth and openness that she had immediately realized her earlier fears had all been for naught.

They were pleased that she had roots in Promise, believing as they did that the town's future prosperity depended on intelligent, well-educated young people like her and Jack who were willing not only to return, but also to contribute of their time and talents.

They didn't seem to mind that there was a baby on the way, either. Jack's mother fairly glowed when she talked about the prospect of finally having a grandchild to spoil. Of course, Elaine had also wanted to know if they'd set a date for the wedding. Left on her own to explain, Abby had said that they were still in the process of deciding.

There had also been the matter of Jack's house— a house Abby had to admit she hadn't yet seen. Elaine seemed incensed on her future daughter-in-law's behalf that Jack hadn't included her in such an important decision. Mentally cursing Jack, who had been out on the patio, helping his father grill the salmon, Abby had said that she was sure she would like the house just fine.

Elaine had eyed her uncertainly, looking as if she were about to say something more on the subject, but the men came in with the platter of sizzling salmon steaks and she went off to toss the salad.

On the drive back to her mother's house later that evening, Jack had asked how she'd enjoyed the evening. She'd had to admit to having a wonderful time with his parents. And she hadn't missed the smug smile tugging at the corners of his mouth as she did so.

Abby saw the same smile on his face the next day when they took her grandparents to the café for Sunday brunch. Hank and Judith greeted Jack as if he really were engaged to their granddaughter, even though Abby had told them the truth about their relationship the previous day.

They hadn't seemed to really believe her Saturday morning when she told them about their pretend engagement and the reasons for it. And with Jack playing the part of devoted suitor, they had seemed to believe her even less on Sunday morning.

Jack had been utterly charming, of course, and her grandparents had gone along with him quite willingly. Twice, she had slipped in a comment about their *temporary* arrangement, and twice, all three of them looked at her as if she were a stubborn, spoiled child who needed to be humored.

Finally, Abby had given up trying to make any of them face the facts. She didn't want Hank and Judith to be hurt when her short *engagement* ended, but she couldn't force them to believe something they didn't want to believe, either.

After they had driven her grandparents back to their apartment, Abby had taken her frustration out on Jack, refusing to let him help with the sorting-out chores she'd set for herself Sunday afternoon. He had gone without argument, but he'd stopped by Monday after work with baked chicken and potato salad from the new deli on the square, seeming to know she'd be too hungry to turn him away.

Tuesday night they had joined his associates at the clinic for dinner at Donald Brooks' house. Wednesday, the announcement of their engagement appeared in the local paper, and Jack had again stopped by after work, this time to celebrate with cartons of Chinese food. Again, Abby hadn't been able to resist his boyish smile or the delectable aromas wafting from the bags he held in his hands.

There was a saying about the way to a man's heart being through his stomach. Obviously, Jack had decided, and rightly so if her drooling response was any indication, that the same was true of the woman carrying his child.

Much to Abby's chagrin, she had to admit that his campaign was beginning to work on her emotions.

They had been together for several hours every day for almost a week now, and each time Jack left her with no more than a chaste kiss on the cheek, Abby was sorrier to see him go.

Either Jack was a master at taking on whatever role he chose, or he honestly and truthfully cherished her the way a man should cherish the woman he was about to marry. For someone only out to protect her good name, he seemed to be going to an awful lot of trouble.

Still, Abby tried to harden her heart to him, her need for self-preservation too great to ignore. No matter how good Jack was at pretending, the situation, as she saw it, remained the same. He had shown his true colors in December, and nothing he said or did now could change that.

Or so Abby insisted on telling herself yet again on Thursday night as she stood beside Jack, waiting patiently while he ordered a glass of ginger ale for her at the bar set up in the grand ballroom of the Gladeway Country Club where his parents were hosting a massive engagement party for their son and future daughter-in-law.

Looking at the milling crowd of people, she realized anybody who was anybody in Promise, Nevada—old-timers and newcomers alike—was there. Even Constance Beckworth had put in an appearance, pausing to tell Abby how lovely she looked before moving off to join friends.

Wearing a purple silk dress suitable for a matron her age, Constance now held court at the table where she'd been seated with several other former bank employees. At another table sat the staff of the clinic, and Jack, bless his heart, had made sure her grandparents would have an especially enjoyable evening by not only making sure some of their old friends were included in the festivities, but also seeing that they were seated all together at one of the more prominent tables.

Blinking at the sudden, unexpected sting of tears in her eyes, Abby lowered her gaze as she twisted the lovely diamond ring round and round on her finger.

"What's wrong?" Jack asked, handing her the glass of ginger ale she'd requested.

"Nothing..." she murmured as she took it from him without meeting his gaze.

"Aren't you having a good time?" He put a hand on her arm and gently guided her to a quiet alcove where several tall palm trees sheltered them from view.

"Yes." Still without looking at him, Abby took a sip of her drink, willing away whatever it was that had her wanting nothing more than to sob her heart out.

"We can leave if you'd like," Jack offered, moving his hand from her arm to her shoulder and giving her a hug.

"But the party has just started." Almost undone by his tenderness, she leaned against him, savoring his solid, steady warmth. "And your parents went to so much trouble for us," she added, finally saying aloud what she had been thinking since she and Jack had arrived at the country club. "Too much trouble and too much expense for a *pretend* engagement."

She smoothed a hand down the skirt of the simple, high-waisted, sleeveless black dress she wore, her ring sparkling in the muted light.

"They love giving parties, and we gave them as good a reason as any," Jack assured her, hugging her again.

"They're going to be so upset, though, when I go back to San Francisco—"

"Don't worry about it. Engagements are broken all the time. If you still want to go back to San Francisco ten days from now, no harm will have been done."

"There's no *if* about it, Jack. You've known that all week, and yet you let your parents do this." Abby waved her hand at the crowd of people, the bar, the brimming buffet tables, the string quartet playing one lilting classical piece after another.

"There was no way I could stop them short of telling the truth," Jack reminded her in a reasonable tone.

"Maybe you should have," Abby countered angrily. "Who, in their right mind—especially in this day and age—*pretends* to be engaged to avoid gossip? Your proposition was ridiculous to start out with. Less than a week later, we've moved into another realm altogether—that of the truly absurd. We can't go on with this charade. At least, *I* can't."

"It's only for another week or so," Jack soothed, rubbing his hand up and down her arm. "Humor me just a little longer. Unless it's been really awful for you…" Putting both hands on her shoulders, he turned her so that she faced him, and looked at her intently. "Has it, Abby? Has being engaged to me been awful for you?"

"No, it hasn't," she admitted. "It's just that it's not real."

"It can be. All you have to do is say the word. Because I—"

"There you are," Jack's father interrupted, joining them in the alcove along with a short, balding man closer to Jack's age. "I've been looking all over for the two of you. Should have known you'd try to sneak away for a few minutes on your own. Time enough for that later, though.

"Right now, I want Abby to meet Jerry Banning. He's the president and CEO of Banningware Products, newly relocated to our humble town. And he's currently seeking a replacement for his chief financial officer who has decided to take early retirement so he can sail around the world.

"I told him about your background and credentials, Abby, and he's very interested. Aren't you, Jerry?"

"Yes, indeed, very interested, Ms. Summers. From what J.B. has told me, you're just the kind of person I'm looking for to take over as Banningware's CFO. With your education and experience, you would be a wonderful addition to our family. Of course, I'm aware that you're going to have a new addition to your own family in a few months, but we're set up in such a way that you could work from home quite easily on whatever schedule suits you best."

"But, Mr. Banning," Abby began, overwhelmed by his offer. "You don't really know me."

"Jerry—call me Jerry. Everybody does. And your future father-in-law has spoken so highly of you that I feel I do know you. Of course, I'll understand if you're not seeking a position here in Promise just yet."

"It's not that," Abby hedged, excited in spite of

herself at the prospect of getting in on the ground floor of a company as promising as Banningware was said to be. "I do have some loose ends to tie up in San Francisco, though."

"No problem. Bert, our current CFO, said he'd hang around until the first of the year, if necessary."

"Jack, Abby...I've been looking for you." Elaine Randall, with Jan Nelson in tow, wedged into the alcove and shook a finger at them. "You're supposed to be mingling with our guests."

"They are," J.B. said. "They're mingling with Jerry, here."

"And talking business, no doubt. Did you get Abby to agree to go to work for you?" Elaine asked.

"I'm working on it," Jerry answered, flashing a smile.

"Good." Elaine patted Jerry on the arm, then made a shooing motion at him and J.B. "Now off with the two of you so Jan can try to talk them into at least thinking about buying another house." As Jerry and J.B. sauntered off, Elaine gave Jan a gentle nudge in Jack and Abby's direction. "Have you seen the place yet, Abby? It needs a lot of work, and with a baby on the way—"

"Actually, I haven't had a chance," Abby cut in, hoping to avoid having to deceive Jack's mother any further.

Beside her, Jack groaned as his mother rounded on him.

"You're afraid to take her out there until after you've signed all the papers, aren't you? She's going to be your wife, young man. She has a right to know what you're getting her into."

"We've both been busy all week," he offered by

way of explanation. "But I'm taking off tomorrow afternoon just so I can take Abby out to see the house. And I swear, if she doesn't like it, we'll find something she does. Won't we, sweetheart?"

Jack gave her arm a gentle, warning squeeze as he smiled into her eyes, and Abby nodded silently, going along with him yet again when all she really wanted to do was stomp her feet and yell "no fair."

"I have a lovely two-story, brick, five-bedroom, three-bath, custom-built home on the golf course just three blocks from your parents coming on the market within the next month or so," Jan advised with a perky smile.

"Not the Drexler house?" Elaine asked, her eyes lighting up, then added, "Bert Drexler is Jerry Banning's CFO, the one who's taking early retirement. Their house is beautiful, inside and out."

"We'll keep that in mind," Jack said, then drew Abby's hand through the crook of his arm. "Now I think maybe I'd better get Abby something to eat. Right, sweetheart?"

Again, Abby nodded wordlessly, too overwhelmed to trust herself to speak coherently. There was a word for what she was allowing to be done to her—that word was *coerced.* And she was going to have to put a stop to it before she found herself walking down the aisle on her way to a *pretend* marriage just to keep all these caring, kind, decent, thoughtful people—including Jack, himself—happy.

She would have a wonderful life as his wife—she could see that already. She would have a family she could depend on and a job she would find fulfilling. But in the back of her mind, she would always know that she had settled for less than she truly deserved.

Because she would always know that Jack was settling, too.

Settling for someone he liked well enough, especially since she was pregnant with his child, but not someone he truly loved the way he had once loved someone else.

"Hey, you're looking pensive again," Jack said as he led her toward the buffet table. "I didn't mean to spring that on you about going out to the house tomorrow. We can put it off till Saturday or Sunday—"

"Oh, no. We might as well go tomorrow. Then I can *pretend* to like the house so you won't have to buy the mansion coming on the market in your parents' neighborhood, instead."

"I wouldn't mind, if that's the kind of house you'd like to have."

"Jack…" Abby began, not even trying to hide her exasperation as she paused and looked up at him. When she saw the mischievous gleam in his eyes, she shook her head despairingly. "You are *incorrigible.*"

"Is that good or bad?"

"Bad, Jack. Very, very, *very* bad. And frustrating, too."

"Good." He grinned and gave her arm a tug. "Now come and have something to eat. There's roast beef, shrimp, ham, salads and veggies galore—all sorts of goodies to satisfy your cravings."

Abby wanted to resist, not only Jack's charm, but the laden buffet table, too. But she was weak in mind and body, craving Jack's company as much as the shrimp and fresh asparagus she piled onto a plate. More, actually.

And since she could satisfy both cravings at once, she went along with him, letting herself pretend—for the rest of the evening, at least—that she was the happiest woman alive.

Only when Jack left her alone at her mother's house late that night did she finally come back down to earth with a crash. He blithely kissed her good-night, then turned and walked away without a backward glance. Because they were just *pretending,* weren't they?

Pride alone kept her from calling him back and begging him to stay. Their relationship really was only make-believe, after all. And make-believe came with certain boundaries. She couldn't expect Jack to cross those pre-set lines, and she most assuredly wouldn't cross them herself.

She would think about San Francisco, instead—her home and her job there. And she would remember that she had a mere ten days left before her fairy-tale romance ended.

Chapter Eighteen

"I really don't think this is necessary," Abby grumbled.

She sat beside Jack in the passenger seat of his car, arms folded across her chest in a way he recognized all too well. At the party last night, she had made it clear that her patience was wearing thin where their *engagement* was concerned, and today her mood was even more recalcitrant.

When first his father and Jerry Banning, then his mother and Jan Nelson, had confronted her with their thoughts on a possible job and a home for her in Promise, Abby had looked like a deer caught in the headlights of a semi-trailer truck. For a while there, Jack had been afraid she would do something crazy—maybe jump up on a table and announce to everyone that they were just kidding about a wedding on the way.

He had managed to tease her out of her mood, but just barely. And he had known, the moment she opened the door to him, that she was anything but eager to continue their charade by going with him to see the house he planned to buy.

Only the fact that Jan Nelson had been waiting at the curb in her own car had convinced Abby to stick with the plan he'd foisted on her the night before. She knew that the real estate agent had set aside a block of her valuable time to show them the property personally, and she was too conscientious to disappoint the cheerfully smiling woman waving a greeting.

Abby had no qualms about making her annoyance known to him, however.

"Look at it this way," Jack suggested for the third time that afternoon, schooling himself to be patient as he followed Jan's lead down the driveway that led to the house he'd chosen to buy. "Once you've seen the place, you can tell everyone you love it, and no one will bother you about it again the rest of the time you're in Promise."

"What if I don't love it?" Abby asked in a sulky tone he had yet to hear her use.

Caught off guard by her sudden, seeming, perversity, Jack pulled to a stop behind Jan's car, shut off the engine, then turned to face Abby.

"Then, my precious darling, we'll ask Jan to find a place for us that you *do* like," he ground out, not even trying to hide his exasperation.

"Okay." Tilting her head, she flashed an impish grin that shot through him like an arrow, straight to his heart.

Jack knew she was just giving him a hard time,

teasing him in much the same way he had teased her last night, but he felt suddenly, unaccountably happy all the same. If she felt comfortable enough with him to behave in such a bedeviling way, then he had most definitely made a measurable amount of progress with her.

Truly heartened for the first time since he had proposed their pretend engagement, Jack put his hands on Abby's shoulders, pulled her as close as he could across the car's center gearshift, and kissed her soundly on the mouth.

When, to his surprise and utter elation, Abby clutched at the fabric of his shirt and kissed him back, it was all he could do to lift his head and ease away from her. Mindful not only of where they were, but that they also had an audience, he drew a steadying breath, then smiled slowly.

"You're a brat, you know," he said, his voice laced with a tenderness that belied his words. "Pouting one minute, then provoking me in a whole other way the next."

"Only because you bring it out in me," Abby advised, tossing him a saucy look as she arched one elegant eyebrow. "And I *wasn't* provoking you."

"You mean you didn't want to be kissed?" Jack feigned surprise. "Sorry, my mistake. I must have just imagined that you were sliding your tongue all over mine..."

"You started it," she accused, her face turning bright red.

"And, unfortunately, I have to finish it for now since Jan's waiting for us." He reached out and curled a wisp of her hair around his finger. "But I'm not letting the moment go completely. Unless I'm sadly mistaken, we've got something here worth exploring in much more detail.''

"Don't be silly. It was only a momentary lapse," Abby said, grabbing the handle of the car door.

"Yeah, sure, and I'm an alien from another planet.''

"Ah, now I know why you were so eager for us to *pretend* to be engaged. Only a real space cadet would have thought of something so nonsensical.''

"Or a man making a last-ditch attempt to win back the regard of the woman he loves,'' Jack countered quietly, bringing an end to their bantering.

He hoped he wouldn't regret being so honest with Abby, but she had given him so few chances to tell her how he really felt about her that he couldn't let this one pass.

Her lips slightly parted, Abby stared at him, wide-eyed, for several seconds, the bright color slowly draining from her face. Then she gave her head a negative shake, as if clearing her mind of unwanted thoughts.

"Don't be silly,'' she said again.

"I'm not. I'm being honest with you.''

"No,'' she stated firmly. "You're just being kind.''

Dismissing anything further he might have said with a wave of her hand, Abby opened the car door, climbed out, then shut it again quickly.

Head bowed over the steering wheel, Jack pounded a fist against his thigh in frustration. He had tried showing Abby how much he cared for her in as gallant and as gentlemanly a way as he knew how, but that had only gotten him so far. And she refused to believe any words of love he worked up the courage to speak aloud.

Time was running out. He had only a little more than a week left before she planned to go back to San Francisco. He was going to have to change his tactics fast or risk losing her for good.

In the moments Jack sat alone in the car, a whole new battle plan began to take shape in his mind. He was going to use the kiss they had just shared as his jumping-off point, and take it from there. Not slowly and carefully as he'd been doing, but gung-ho, alpha-male all the way.

He and Abby had been good together the night they'd made love—so very, very good together. Abby had obviously chosen to forget that, but her memory could easily be refreshed. He had limited himself to leaving her with chaste kisses on the cheek long enough.

Tonight, he wasn't leaving her at all.

Spurred on by a new sense of determination, Jack got out of the car and sauntered over to where Abby stood, chattering nervously to Jan Nelson about how lovely the property looked with the grass so lush and the fruit trees blooming. The real estate agent flicked a questioning glance his way, but he ignored her, choosing instead to put a proprietary arm around Abby's shoulders.

She tensed at his touch, and when she looked up at him, her smile was somewhat lacking in sincerity, but Jack didn't let it bother him. He had tiptoed around Abby long enough, muttering his mea culpas. It would do her good to be a little wary of him now.

He wanted her to wonder what he was up to until the moment he swept her off her feet and carried her to bed. He was going to take her by surprise, and turn her every way but loose. Then, finally, she would have to—

"We had better go inside," Jan said, interrupting his reverie. She gestured to the darkening sky off to the west and added, "It looks like the storm they mentioned on the news this morning is definitely headed our way, and I'd like to get back to town before it hits."

"Good idea," Jack agreed. "Lead the way."

With his arm still around Abby's shoulders, drawing her along beside him, he followed Jan to the porch that ran the length of the stone and wood-frame ranch house. She unlocked the door for them, then waved them into the small entryway.

"I have a couple of calls to make on my cell phone, so why don't you show Abby around?" she said.

The house was cool and welcoming, at least to Jack. He couldn't judge by Abby's expression how she felt about it. She didn't say much, either, as he walked with her through the large, open rooms, their footsteps on the Saltillo tile and hardwood floors echoing in the emptiness.

She paused by the long bank of windows overlooking the back garden and the orchard beyond for quite a while, and she prowled around the big, old-fashioned kitchen, opening cabinet and pantry doors. He caught her smiling at the claw-footed bathtubs as she ran her fingertips over the green-and-yellow tile work in the bathrooms. And she sat in the window seat of the master bedroom for several seconds, again looking out at the back garden and orchard.

Two of the other three bedrooms she gave only a

cursory glance, but the third bedroom with its small built-in desk and floor-to-ceiling bookshelves along one wall held her attention much longer. Jack had planned to use the room as a home office, but he would willingly let Abby have it, should she take Jerry Banning up on his offer of a job. He had an office at the clinic, after all. And they could always add on as their family grew.

"Well, what do you think?" Jan asked, joining them again as they returned to the large, L-shaped living area at the house's center.

"I really like it," Abby said, sounding not only surprised, but a little wistful, as well. "It needs paint and wallpaper, of course, and new appliances in the kitchen, but otherwise…" She paused, glanced at Jack, then quickly away again. "I can see why you chose it. Even with the sky so overcast, there's a lot of light in here, and the rooms are so open and inviting. It would be fun to entertain here."

"It *will* be fun," Jack amended. "We should have the place presentable long before the baby comes. We can have an open house then, and invite all of our family and friends."

"So, you want me to go ahead with the loan application?" Jan asked.

"Abby?" Jack deferred to her with an encouraging smile.

She eyed him with sudden panic, obviously unwilling to have to cast the deciding vote about a house she wasn't really planning to inhabit.

"You *will* be happy here, won't you?" Jack pressed. "That matters more than anything, you know."

"Yes," Abby said, looking away. "Yes, I'd be happy here."

"Well, then, that's all settled," Jan chirped. "Now, we'd best be going or we'll never beat the rain back to town. Unless you want to stay a little longer, maybe talk about the paint and wallpaper changes you'd like to make. I'll be happy to leave the keys with you. You can lock up whenever you're ready…"

"Oh, no," Abby replied so adamantly that Jan gave her a curious look.

"Not today," Jack added, smoothly distracting the agent. "I'd like to get back to town, too. We have plans for later."

Abby shot him a "what plans?" glance, but he ignored her as they walked to the entryway with Jan. They had just stepped onto the front porch when a streak of lightning lit up the sky, followed almost immediately by a crash of thunder. Jan quickly locked the door, then waved a hand at them.

"I'm out of here. Talk to you again in a few days," she said, hurrying to her car as the first powerful wave of rain swept across the lawn.

"Thanks for coming out here with us," Jack called after her as he took Abby by the arm and headed for his car.

Since they were parked farther away, and Jack walked more slowly with Abby so she wouldn't trip on the uneven ground, the two of them were all but drenched by the time they reached his car. Inside at last, he grabbed an old blanket off the back seat that he kept handy for emergencies and put it around Abby's shoulders. Using a roll of paper towels, he mopped off his face and arms as best he could, then started the engine.

"That was wicked of you, Jack Randall," Abby said once they were under way.

"What was?" he asked, peering through the foggy windshield as a gust of wind buffeted the car.

"Asking me if I'd be happy in the house with Jan standing there."

"She would have been surprised if I hadn't. After all, we were there to get your opinion of the house, and I wanted to know, too."

"Why? I'm not going to actually be living there."

"Oops," Jack muttered, momentarily distracted as the car hit a patch of water pooling in a low spot on the road and swerved a bit.

"I'm sorry," Abby said. "With the weather so bad, I should let you concentrate on driving, shouldn't I?"

"Right. We'll talk more once we're back at your mother's house."

"Part of our plans for the evening?" she couldn't seem to help but ask, her tone sardonic.

"Not the talking, no. But we can do that too, if you'd like."

From the corner of his eye, Jack saw Abby looking at him somewhat askance, and smiled to himself. Then he focused his full attention on the road, determined to get Abby home safely so he could have his wicked way with her, at last.

Chapter Nineteen

The storm had brought with it a drop in air temperature. Even wrapped in the old blanket with the car's heater blasting hot air in her face, Abby couldn't seem to get warm on the drive back to her mother's house. Her braid hung wet and heavy against the back of her neck, her T-shirt and shorts clung to her skin, and her sodden sneakers squished uncomfortably on her icy feet. No matter how she tried, she couldn't stop the shivers running up and down her spine.

Beside her, Jack wasn't in much better shape. He was just as wet despite the blotting he'd given himself with the paper towels, and he didn't have the benefit of a blanket to huddle under. Goose bumps covered his arms and legs where they stuck out from the short sleeves of his shirt and the hem of his shorts. Only the tight grip of his hands on the steering wheel eased his own shivers, and then, just the tiniest bit.

Since they had pulled onto the main highway into town, he hadn't said anything, keeping his attention focused on the road ahead. He drove slowly, in deference to the pouring rain and gusty wind, avoiding as best he could the puddles of water already standing on the pavement.

They rarely had such heavy rain in Promise, but when they did, it wasn't unusual for the roads to flood temporarily. Fortunately, there weren't many other vehicles out in the storm, and the drivers of those that were seemed to be moving along as cautiously as Jack.

"Not too much longer and I'll have you home," he said as they passed the Promise city limit sign, barely discernible in the continuing downpour.

"G-g-good," she stuttered through chattering teeth.

"You've caught a chill, haven't you?" He took a hand from the steering wheel and gave her arm a quick squeeze.

"Y-y-you, t-t-too," she replied, feeling the tremor in his touch.

"A hot shower should warm you up fast."

"Mmm…" Just the thought made Abby groan with anticipation. "Y-y-you, t-t-too," she said again.

"Oh, yeah, me, *definitely,* too," Jack agreed, his voice dropping into the same sexy tonal range he had used when he'd commented on his plans for the evening at the start of their drive home.

As Abby's heartbeat quickened noticeably, she warned herself not to let her imagination run wild. Whatever Jack might have in mind for them tonight, it wasn't going to involve anything...intimate. At least, not if she had any say in the matter.

She knew how easily Jack could lure her into doing something she'd end up regretting. He had done just that in December. She fully intended to say a firm and uncompromising *no* to anything that even *seemed* likely to go beyond the chaste kisses he'd been giving her the past week. Regardless of how bereft she would feel.

She had made a big mistake kissing him back earlier—especially with such obviously wanton enthusiasm. She had led him on in a way she now rued.

They were not really engaged, they were not getting married, and they most certainly were not going to live happily ever after in the house she had absolutely, positively fallen in love with that afternoon. She was going back to San Francisco in ten days, and she wasn't going to let Jack do anything more than he already had to tempt her to change her mind.

"Here we are," he said, drawing her back to the present moment as he pulled into the driveway. "Looks like we're going to have to make a run for the front door. Do you have your key handy?"

Abby wanted to tell him there was no need for him to see her to the door and get even wetter himself, only to have to continue on to his apartment. She was perfectly capable of letting herself into the house on her own.

But she couldn't do that to Jack. He was obviously chilled to the bone already. Refusing to allow him to stay with her until he'd had a chance to dry off would be too cruel, especially when he was so concerned about her. The least she could do was invite him inside and offer him the use of her shower, her terry-cloth robe, and a hot cup of tea while his clothes tumbled in the dryer.

"Right here," she said, making up her mind as she fished her door key from her purse and handed it to him.

"I want you to stay put until I unlock the door and come back for you, okay? I don't want you to risk slipping on a patch of wet grass and landing on your bottom."

"Okay," Abby agreed.

By the time they were both safely inside the house, they were also wetter than ever. Even using the old blanket as a partial shield from the torrential downpour had done them little good.

Dropping her end of the blanket in the entryway, Abby scraped the dripping tendrils of hair away from her face, then tried to wipe the moisture from her eyes with her fingertips. Jack, too, let go of the blanket, allowing it to drop in a sodden heap on the floor, then shook his head like a shaggy dog in a seemingly futile attempt to get the water out of his eyes, as well.

Though it was warmer in the house than it had been outside—thanks to Abby's thrifty habit of raising the thermostat on the air conditioner before she left—it wasn't by much. She couldn't seem to stop shivering even when she ran her hands briskly up and down her arms.

Jack noticed at once. Putting an arm around her shoulders, he started walking her toward the hallway that led to the house's only bathroom.

"Let's get you into a hot shower or you're going to end up with pneumonia," he said.

"No, you go first," Abby protested. "Just hand me a couple of towels so I can—"

"Don't be silly," Jack cut in. "I'm not nearly as chilled as you are, and I'm not pregnant, either. If I end up catching a cold, it's no big deal. But if you do, the baby will be affected, too."

Aware that arguing with him would not only be ridiculous, but also futile, Abby gratefully kicked off her sneakers while Jack started the water running. She reached for the waistband of her shorts, then hesitated as he glanced back at her.

"Uh, I can take it from here," she murmured.

"Okay, I'll go drip all over the living room." He flashed a wry grin as he turned away.

"Wait...take some towels." Feeling like a thankless wretch, Abby opened the linen cabinet, grabbed several bath towels and handed them to Jack. "You can wrap up in my robe, too, and put your clothes in the dryer." She reached behind the door for her oversize white terry-cloth robe and tossed it atop the pile of towels. "I promise I won't be long."

"Don't hurry on my account. I'd rather you take your time. Make sure you're good and warm before you get out from under the hot water."

"I will," Abby assured him as he finally backed out of the bathroom, pulling the door closed as he did.

Once she heard the latch click, Abby didn't waste a moment peeling off her soaking wet clothes, letting them fall in a pile on the floor, then stepping under the steamy hot spray of the shower. As the moist heat began to chase away the icy chill that had penetrated to her very bones, she sighed blissfully and closed her eyes.

The rustle of the shower curtain a few moments later, however, had her suddenly staring wide-eyed through the thick mist at a bare, well-muscled chest, a pair of broad shoulders, a square chin, a smiling mouth and teasingly sexy green eyes.

"Jack...what are you doing?" Abby demanded, backing up against the tile wall, the last word coming out of her mouth as more of a squeak than anything.

"I thought I could tough it out and wait until you were finished in here, but I was too wet and too cold. Call me a wimp if you want, but here I am." He reached out and touched her cheek. "You don't really mind, do you? There's more than enough room for the two of us."

Suddenly aware that she was standing there, stark naked, Abby folded her arms over her breasts.

"Actually, I'm...I'm all done," she said, trying, unsuccessfully, to ease past him.

"But you've only been in here a couple of minutes. Not even enough time to soap up." Solidly blocking her way out of the shower stall, Jack reached for the bar of soap in the soap dish and started rubbing up a lather in his hands. "Turn around and I'll start with your back."

Abby could have blustered her way past him...if she had really wanted to. Jack wouldn't have kept her in the shower stall against her will. But standing under the steamy spray, watching his clever hands making glorious wads of bubbles from a simple bar of lavender-scented soap, she felt too weak of body, mind and spirit to do anything but turn obediently and let him do as he'd offered.

At least she was saved from the temptation of brazenly lowering her gaze, or worse, simply taking a step or two closer to him, putting her arms around him and rubbing up against him invitingly like a sex-starved hussy.

Which she most certainly was, but oh, well...

The feel of Jack's hands on her back, slick with soap as they massaged their way from her shoulders to her hips had her arching her neck and sighing deeply in a matter of seconds. And when those same delightfully inventive hands eased around to cover her breasts, she sucked in a deep, audible breath, not of surprise, but of undisguised pleasure.

Bending close, Jack whispered in her ear as he quickly loosened his grip, "Sorry, I didn't mean to hurt you."

"You didn't." Reaching up, she pressed his hands to her more firmly, once again. "My breasts are just super-sensitive. Apparently it's a normal part of pregnancy."

"Do you like it?" he asked, nuzzling the side of her neck.

"I do now," she murmured in reply.

Using one hand to tease at her nipples, Jack skimmed the other down along her rib cage, then splayed his palm across the growing mound of her belly.

"Getting bigger," he said, the pride and protectiveness in his voice evident.

"Mmm, yes. Moving around more and more, too."

It felt so natural to Abby, standing there with Jack's hands on her body, talking about their baby. As if they had been together for years instead of just a few days.

"Boy or girl?" he asked, his thumb toying with the little indent of her belly button.

"I'm only asking for healthy. Then I'll be happy, no matter what," she admitted.

"Me, too."

Drawing her back against his chest so that she could feel the evidence of his desire, he pressed an openmouthed kiss on the back of her neck and moved his hand lower still.

Gasping, Abby spread her legs, then reached down and guided his fingers right where she wanted them, *needed* them. With the softest, sexiest, most masculine of chuckles, Jack obliged her quite deftly, delving into her with such masterful strokes that he soon had her writhing in his arms like a wild thing.

"Jack...oh, Jack...please," she begged, her voice husky as she tipped her head back against his shoulder.

"Now?" His eyes gleamed mischievously as he feathered a kiss on her lips.

"Yes, now...*now,*" she wailed, the hard length of his body supporting her, the light dip and rub of his fingertips, the hot, steamy spray of water beating against her all combining to shift her senses into overload.

Jack increased the pressure of his thumb on her as he took her mouth in a deep, drugging kiss, eating the cry that came from her with her release.

So weak in the knees that she could barely stand, Abby turned in his arms and sagged against him, holding on to him as she tried to steady her breathing.

"Better?" he asked, reaching around her to turn off the faucet.

"Oh, yes. But you...you—"

"Don't worry, sweetheart. We're far from finished yet."

Jack's eyes gleamed with such deviltry as he shoved aside the shower curtain that Abby's knees threatened to give out all over again. Steadying her with a hand on her arm, he helped her step onto the bath mat, then took one of the towels he'd left on the counter and quickly dried her off.

"Now you," she said when he had finished, grabbing a fresh towel so she could return the favor.

"Mmm, nice. I could get used to this," he muttered as she scrubbed the soft terry cloth down his broad chest and over his belly.

"Me, too," Abby admitted, moving the towel lower, teasing it along the rigid length of him.

"Enough," Jack ground out in a tormented voice.

He caught her hands in his, took the towel from her and dropped it on the floor, then scooped her into his arms and carried her down the hallway to her bedroom.

Outside the house, the rain continued to fall, though not with quite so thunderous a roar. Inside, Abby's bedroom was a dimly lit and cozy cave, her narrow bed a place where she and Jack could once again set aside all their inhibitions. As they had that night in December, they came together as equal partners, each giving and taking in the same measure.

With her guard lowered and her defenses down, Abby reveled in the pleasure of their mating, meeting Jack's thrusts with an urgency that belied her earlier satisfaction. And afterward, lying in his arms as he held her close, so close to his heart, she could almost believe again, as she had in December, that surely he must love her—really, truly *love* her.

The tenderness he had shown her when he'd put his mouth to her could not be faked. Nor could the passion with which he had called her name at the moment of his release, or the wonderment when he nuzzled her neck and murmured, "You're everything to me...everything...Abby Summers."

She wanted those moments to last forever, but unfortunately, her tummy had other ideas, growling so loudly that she couldn't help but giggle self-consciously.

"Hungry?" Jack chuckled, too, then gave her a comforting hug.

"Much as I hate to admit it, yes," Abby answered.

"Well, it *is* dinnertime." He stretched as best he could in the narrow bed, then splayed his hand across her belly. "And you are eating for two."

"I'm beginning to wonder if I'm actually eating for three or four," she admitted ruefully.

"Is it possible? Twins...or even triplets?" Jack levered up on an elbow and looked down at her, his expression such a mixture of panic and delight that she couldn't help but smile.

"Not this time. I had a sonogram just before I left San Francisco, and the doctor assured me there is only one baby growing inside me."

"Well, then, maybe next time," Jack teased. "The older we get, the more chance we'll have for a multiple birth."

He sounded so enthusiastic about the prospect of a future pregnancy that Abby couldn't bring herself to burst his bubble by reminding him that they weren't actually going to live happily ever after as husband and wife.

Or maybe she didn't want to burst her own bubble.

She, too, liked the idea of having a houseful of children with Jack Randall. In fact, she wanted that so much, lying there with him, that she had to let herself trust in the possibility, at least for what remained of their magical night together.

"I can't believe you're talking about *next* time when I still have most of *this* time ahead of me," she said.

"Ahead of *us*," Jack reminded her, giving her another hug. "Now, what about dinner? It sounds like the rain is letting up. Do you want to go out?"

"I'd really rather stay in, unless—"

"I'd like that better, too. So, we'll stay in."

"I have all the fixings for a really monster omelet on hand, and there are some of my grandmother's homemade biscuits in the freezer. How does breakfast for dinner sound to you?"

"Perfect."

With Jack looking rather cute in her old terry-cloth robe, and Abby feeling sexy in her short, royal blue silk robe, they bumped around the kitchen together, laughing and talking like a couple of old married people as they prepared their omelet.

And later, with the dishes done and the evening stretching ahead of them, they drifted back to her bedroom, one as eager as the other to pick up where they'd left off, alternately playful and intense in their lovemaking until, exhausted at last, they curled close, arms around each other, and slept.

The last thing Jack wanted to do Saturday morning was leave Abby alone. The last time he'd done so, there had been hell to pay, and he didn't want to risk having history repeat itself. He had traded the hours he'd taken off from the clinic Friday afternoon for Aaron Post's Saturday morning hours, however, so he had no choice but to show up there.

Jack would have much preferred spending the early hours of the day snuggled close to Abby, finally making serious plans with her for their future together. She had to realize how much he loved her now—as much as, if not more than, he had loved her that fateful night in December.

But he wanted to tell her, face-to-face, in the clear light of a new day, so that any lingering doubts she might have would finally be put to rest. After last night, Abby wouldn't be able to tell herself that his only real interest in her revolved around the baby, and Jack wanted to make sure that she could admit it, once and for all.

He had kept her up half the night, making love to her, though. As a result, she was sleeping so soundly that it seemed criminal to wake her only to tell her that he had to leave. And leave he must if he wanted to be at the clinic by eight o'clock.

He had to go by his apartment, take a shower, dress, and eat something, all in just over an hour. He would be free again by early afternoon, though, and he intended to come back here. He and Abby could talk just as well then as now. All he had to do was leave a note telling her what he had in mind.

In the kitchen, Jack retrieved his wrinkled shorts and T-shirt from the dryer and pulled them on. Then he found paper and a pen in the same place he had that night in December.

But the note he wrote to Abby this time was as different from the note he'd written then as night from day. In this note, he promised to be back soon to say to her all the things he should have said in December. And instead of leaving it on the kitchen table, Jack took it back to her bedroom and propped it on the nightstand where she would be sure to see it as soon as she awakened.

Tucking the bedcovers up around her shoulders, Jack smiled down at her, his heart swelling with a mixture of relief and reverence so intense that tears stung his eyes.

He had come so close to ruining all that they could have together out of his groundless fears and uncertainty. But he had been lucky. Abby had given him a second chance. And he was going to do everything in his power to make sure she would never regret it.

Chapter Twenty

Abby awoke to the sound of a car engine turning over and knew at once that it must be Jack leaving for the clinic. Before they had finally fallen asleep, he had said something—actually groaned something—about having to go to work in the morning. So she knew, too, that he wasn't fleeing out of fear as he had said he'd done in December.

Though even if he hadn't mentioned the hours he had to put in at the clinic she wouldn't have thought that history was repeating itself. Not after last night…

As she had that long-ago morning in December, Abby lay alone in her narrow bed, her muscles just the slightest bit stiff, perhaps even a tad sore, from the rigors of her lovemaking with Jack. *Delightful* rigors, she thought, smiling as she stretched her arms over her head languidly, remembering how he had touched her here, kissed her there, and there, and *there*. Recalling, too, the words he had spoken as he'd held her close.

You are everything to me…everything…Abby Summers.

She had believed him in those wondrous moments of afterglow. Had believed, finally, that she had a place all her own in his heart. A place where Abby, just Abby—the woman she was now, not the old friend or the mother of his child—was, and always would be, cherished.

Stretching again, Abby rolled to her side, her smile widening as she felt the baby move deep inside her. On the nightstand, propped against the base of the lamp, was a single sheet of paper, folded once.

From Jack, of course, she thought with a momentary pang of trepidation. Hard to forget the wording of the last note he had left for her. But this one would be different. After last night, it had to be.

And it was, Abby saw at once as she sat up and unfolded the sheet of paper. He would be finished at the clinic by one o'clock at the latest, he had written in his distinctively bold strokes. Then he would come back to the house. Could she please be there? He had something important to say to her—something he should have said in December, and now wanted to say in person.

Holding the note close to her heart, Abby blinked at the sudden sting of tears in her eyes. Last night he had said she was everything to him. And he had shown her, in the most intimate ways possible, that he loved her.

But he hadn't actually spoken those three words aloud—words that were undeniably magical in

meaning and so utterly filled with promise. He hadn't
taken her hands in his, looked her solemnly in the
eye, and said, "I love you." But he would say it to
her that afternoon, and she would say it back to him.
And they would live happily ever after as she had
dreamed of for so long.

There wouldn't be any more need of pretending.
Once spoken aloud and acknowledged, their love for
each other would finally be as real, as lasting and as
true as the diamond ring she so proudly wore.

Folding Jack's note carefully, Abby tucked it into
the drawer of the nightstand, then slipped out of bed,
grabbed her robe and headed for the bathroom. She
took her time in the shower, remembering the feel of
Jack's hands on her as she lathered her lavender soap
on a washcloth and smoothed it over her skin.

Her breasts were more tender than ever after all
the attention Jack had given them. So, too, the junc-
ture of her thighs, but not to an uncomfortable de-
gree. Their lovemaking had been intense, but Jack
had been incredibly gentle with her.

Abby also decided to wash her hair. She had un-
woven her braid after they'd eaten dinner last night,
but Jack hadn't given her time to do much else. Her
damp hair had dried in a tangled mess that made her
look like a wild woman.

Not a bad look, really, she thought with a smile.
But one better suited to lascivious nights than demure
days.

Abby's stomach growled demandingly as she finished drying her hair, and she dressed quickly in a
white T-shirt and her denim jumper. Becoming
enough for the afternoon ahead with Jack, but also

serviceable enough for the task she'd set for herself during the morning hours.

As she poured juice into a glass, then cereal and milk into a bowl and put the kettle on to boil for a cup of tea, Abby acknowledged that she'd put off going through her mother's things long enough.

Larissa's will and the deed to her house had been kept in Hank and Judith's safe deposit box, so retrieving those documents hadn't required a search through the file box full of papers Abby knew her mother had stashed on a closet shelf.

Abby assumed she would find little, if anything, of importance in the file box—more than likely filled with copies of old income tax returns, receipts and appliance warranties, and bank statements. But she wanted to sort through everything just in case.

Her mother could have had a savings account or a certificate of deposit she had forgotten to mention to Abby or Judith. There might be an old photograph of Abby's father tucked away in the box, as well. Maybe even something that would give her a clue to his name.

First, though, she would pack up Larissa's clothes in the boxes Hank had brought over for her the other day so they could be donated, along with Abby's things, to Promise's church-sponsored family ministry program.

Abby had finished her breakfast and just gotten a start emptying out Larissa's dresser drawers when the doorbell rang. Grateful for any diversion from her heartachingly sad task, Abby glanced at the clock on the nightstand and saw that it was just past ten o'clock. She wasn't expecting anyone, but perhaps her grandparents had decided to stop by to give her a hand. She had insisted it wasn't necessary when they offered, but they had known how much she'd been dreading going through her mother's personal effects.

It could be Jan Nelson, too. She might have someone interested in looking at the house. Though she had promised she would call first before bringing anyone over.

Better yet, it could be Jack. Maybe he hadn't been needed at the clinic as long as he'd expected.

Abby hurried to the front door, smiling in anticipation. She didn't even bother to look through the little peep hole to see who was outside before she reached for the knob.

As she swung the door wide, however, and her gaze fell upon the two young women standing on the porch, her smile faded quickly. She was beyond surprised by their appearance. Shocked, actually, and more than a little confused. Looking at them was almost like looking in the mirror.

Although their auburn hair was styled differently than her own, and each other's, they were the same height as she, they had the same blue eyes and the same facial features. They also looked to be the same age as she. And they were dressed in much the same colors she favored, as well as the same style of clothing she had tended to wear before her pregnancy.

They could have easily passed for sisters, the three of them. More than that, they looked so much alike they could have been triplets—identical triplets. But that was impossible, wasn't it?

Who were these women, and what were they doing here, looking at her with such surprise?

Feeling dizzy enough to brace a hand on the door

frame, Abby blinked several times in the vague hope that she was hallucinating. Though why that would have been a preferable alternative she couldn't say.

"My goodness," murmured the one with chin-length curls, wearing a long, slim khaki skirt and green knit shirt.

"My goodness, indeed," agreed the other, dressed in tailored, pale gray slacks and a sleeveless white cotton shirt, her longer hair waving softly around her shoulders.

Abby echoed their comments silently, not quite able to find her voice yet.

"No wonder your neighbor looked at us as if she were seeing a ghost," the first woman added, gesturing toward Constance Beckworth's house.

Glancing past her visitors, Abby noted that Constance was now standing on the sidewalk in front of the house, staring blatantly at the scene unfolding before her.

"Uh, maybe you'd better come inside," she said, her voice sounding oddly unfamiliar to her as she took a step back.

The two women murmured their agreement and entered as Abby directed. Still feeling a bit unsteady, Abby offered them a seat on the sofa, then sat on the chair across from them. She should probably offer them something to drink, but it would be a few minutes before she would be able to get up again.

"We should introduce ourselves," the woman with the shorter hair said. "I'm Sarah Daniels."

"And I'm Jessica Walker," the other woman chimed in, then added tentatively, "We were told Larissa Summers used to live in this house."

"Yes, she did. She was my mother. She died in

December. I'm her daughter. Abby…Abby Summers," Abby replied.

The two women exchanged a glance, then looked back at her, their expressions mirroring Abby's own inner turmoil.

"Larissa Summers was our mother, too," Sarah offered quietly.

"We only just met ourselves, Sarah and I," Jessica continued. "We…we thought we were twins who had somehow been separated at birth when our mother, Larissa, gave us up for adoption. But there were three of us, weren't there? Unless we're not the same age…"

"I'll be twenty-seven on May thirtieth," Abby said.

Sarah and Jessica exchanged another glance, then Jessica nodded her head.

"That's my birthday, too. Sarah was never sure of the exact date, but she always celebrated her birthday at the end of May, as well. So we *are* triplets and we *were* separated at birth."

"Now all we have to do is figure out the how and why," Sarah added with a wry smile. "Obviously, you didn't know about us until today, and we didn't know about you, either."

"We came to Promise because we wanted to find out as much as we could about our birth mother," Jessica explained, picking up where Sarah left off. "We were told she was dead, but we thought maybe we could track down someone who could help us solve the mystery of how we happened to be separated. And here you are, Abby—our sister. And you not only grew up in Promise; you were also raised by our mother."

"But I'm just as confused as you are," Abby admitted. "I never had any idea that I had sisters, much less that I was one of identical triplets."

Another wave of dizziness had her sitting back in the chair. Instinctively, she put a protective hand on the gentle swell of her belly.

"Are you all right?" Jessica asked, moving from the sofa to kneel beside her.

Sarah, too, stood and crossed the room to stand beside her.

"Maybe we should come back later," she suggested. "This whole situation has to be even more overwhelming for you than it has been for us, especially in your condition."

"No, please stay. I'll be fine," Abby insisted, unwilling to be left alone with so many seemingly unanswerable questions.

What on earth had happened to Larissa all those years ago? Because surely *something* had happened. Otherwise why would she have given up two of her three infant daughters?

The decision couldn't have been an easy one for her to make. She must have believed she had no other choice. Larissa might not have been the most traditional of mothers, but she had loved Abby in her own way despite her constant restiveness and discontent.

Brought on, no doubt, by the anguish and the hidden torment of what she had done...

"Can I get you anything?" Jessica offered. "A cold drink, maybe?"

"No, thanks." Abby tried to smile reassuringly, then gestured toward the kitchen. "You're welcome to help yourselves to something, though. I'd serve you myself, but I'm still feeling a bit unsteady.''

"And no wonder," Sarah said. "When is your baby due?''

"The end of September," Abby answered as her sisters moved back to the sofa again. She hesitated a moment, then gave in to her growing curiosity. "Would you mind telling me a little bit about yourselves and how you found each other? My mother— *our* mother—never talked about the time when we were born, and she told me hardly anything about…about our father. All I really know is that she left Las Vegas with me when I was less than a month old and brought me home to her parents here in Promise.

"But maybe your stories might jog some old, forgotten memory of mine. I could have overheard her telling someone something that didn't mean anything to me at the time, but might help us put together the puzzle pieces now.''

"Our father was Lawrence Walker," Jessica began after a nod from Sarah. "He was killed in a plane crash before we were born. Apparently, Larissa was his mistress. My adoptive mother, Deidre Walker, was Lawrence's wife.

"According to her, she somehow found out that Larissa was pregnant. She offered to adopt me and raise me in the Walker family with the support of our grandfather, Stuart Walker, at his home in Willow Springs, Nevada. When Sarah showed up in Willow Springs a few weeks ago, Deidre said she hadn't known a second baby had been born. Or, obviously, a third…''

"I was abandoned at a hospital in Bellville, Nevada, a small town about halfway between Las Vegas and Willow Springs,'' Sarah continued with her story as Abby looked from one to the other, trying to take in all she was hearing. ''Apparently, I had a severe respiratory infection and was very ill for several weeks. When I finally recovered, I was placed in foster care, then adopted by an older couple, Alice and Edward Daniels, after a search for my birth parents proved to be fruitless.

''They died within a few months of each other while I was in college. I've been on my own, more or less, ever since then. At least, until a few weeks ago.''

When Sarah traded glances with Jessica again, they shared a knowing smile that piqued Abby's curiosity even more.

''What?'' she asked, wanting desperately to be included.

They were her sisters—the sisters she had secretly, unknowingly, longed for almost as long as she could remember. To feel like an outsider now that they had finally found each other was doubly difficult.

''You *won't* believe how Sarah and I found each other, Abby,'' Jessica said, turning to her with the same warm smile she'd just shared with Sarah. ''We've proven that truth *is* stranger than fiction, haven't we?''

''Oh, yes, we most certainly have,'' Sarah agreed.

''So, tell me,'' Abby pleaded, scooting to the edge of her chair in barely contained anticipation.

''Go on, Sarah. You first,'' Jessica instructed.

''I was about to be married, literally. One minute, I was putting on my wedding dress, wondering whether I was really in love with my groom-to-be, and the next minute, a crazy man by the name of Ryan Noble barged into my life, insisting that I couldn't marry anyone but him.

"He whisked me away to his cabin in the mountains, sure that I was his fiancée, Jessica, whom he hardly knew. She had been missing for several weeks and Ryan had hired a private investigator to find her. The poor man found me, instead. By the time Ryan took me back to the Walker mansion in Willow Springs and discovered that I wasn't Stuart's heiress granddaughter, and thus not his intended fiancée, we had fallen in love."

Pausing, Sarah looked down at the engagement ring she wore on her left hand and smiled radiantly.

"Jessica was still missing, of course, and Deidre was beside herself with worry. Finding her became our top priority, and though she didn't make it easy for us, we finally did, didn't we?"

Sarah shot Jessica a wry smile, and Jessica nodded ruefully.

"Yes, you certainly did." Jessica looked at Abby, her blue eyes sparkling mischievously. "Ryan is a wonderful man, mind you. He just wasn't the man for me. So, mature woman that I am, when Deidre insisted that I marry him to please Stuart, I decided to run away from home.

"I ended up in Thunder Lake, Nevada with barely two nickels to rub together. Mother had canceled my credit cards and locked up my bank accounts so I had to find a job fast. After a majorly disastrous stint as a waitress, I hired on as nanny for the town sheriff's two little girls.

"Long story short, I fell in love with Sam Dawson and his daughters, Casey and Annie, and fortunately, they fell in love with me, too. Before we could make it official, though, Sarah showed up in Thunder Lake. I returned to Willow Springs with her. That's when we found out from Deidre that she had traced Larissa to Promise, but unfortunately, she had died in an automobile accident in December.

"That sad news was tempered somewhat by Sam's arrival in Willow Springs. He proposed to me, and of course, I accepted." Jessica, too, gazed at the lovely ring she wore before adding, "Sarah and I decided a double wedding was in order, but first we wanted to make a personal trip to Promise—secretly so as not to upset Deidre. We both agreed that we really *needed* to find out as much as we could about our birth mother before we could go on with our lives."

"We left Willow Springs yesterday morning," Sarah explained. "We told everyone we were going to San Francisco to do some shopping, but we headed down here, instead. The drive took us much longer than we expected because we ran into some bad weather. We didn't get to Promise until late, so we found a motel and settled in for the night."

"We called the house in Willow Springs, too," Jessica added. "We thought we'd better tell everyone where we really were. Poor Deidre…she sounded like she was on the verge of hysterics. Fortunately, Grandfather was there to calm her down. I knew there was a good chance we would hurt her feelings by coming here. I never thought she would start shrieking at me like a maniac, though."

"Has anything we've said rung any bells for you?" Sarah asked hopefully.

"Not really," Abby admitted. "To be perfectly

frank, I'm more bewildered than ever. Larissa had her faults, but she never, ever, gave me cause to doubt that she loved me. And knowing her as I did, I'm sure she loved both of you just as much.

"She always seemed to be searching for something. She was so restless and so unhappy. Now I know why. Secretly, she must have been searching for you, deep in her heart, and as long as she couldn't find you, she could never be truly happy."

"Do you really think that was true, Abby?" Jessica asked, tears welling in her eyes. "Do you think Larissa wanted Sarah and me as much as she wanted you? You're the one she kept, after all…"

"Only because she must not have thought she had any choice," Abby insisted. "Her parents, Hank and Judith, were far from wealthy. Asking them to take in one baby was probably as much as she thought she had a right to do. Although they would have welcomed all of us, she wouldn't have wanted to burden them. And she could have thought that we would all have a better life if she and her parents didn't have to bear the full financial responsibility for three tiny babies."

"We wanted to believe that she really did have our best interests at heart when she gave us away," Sarah said, dabbing at her eyes with a tissue.

"She was that kind of person," Abby stated unequivocally. "What puzzles me, though, is why she didn't ask Deidre to adopt both of you. Even if you were ill, Sarah, surely Deidre would have been willing to provide the medical care you needed.

"Since Larissa was willing to entrust her with the care of one of her babies, why not let her have both of you? Even though Larissa couldn't keep all of us, at least she would have known that the two of you were together. That sounds more like something she would have done, rather than abandon Sarah at a hospital.

"A hospital so far from Las Vegas and Promise, too…" Abby added musingly. "I wonder what she was doing in Bellville, Nevada, of all places, with two newborn babies, one of them seriously ill?"

"Maybe she had decided she wanted to keep all of us, after all," Jessica suggested, her expression brightening noticeably. "Maybe she was trying to catch up with Deidre to get me back."

"Or maybe she wanted Stuart to know he had *three* granddaughters," Sarah said. "Larissa could have thought, and rightly so, that he would be able to help her financially."

"Larissa may have been trying to get Jessica back, but I don't think she was trying to contact Stuart. She wouldn't have been able to because she never knew our father's real name," Abby explained. "I remember once overhearing her tell my grandmother that she had tried to find him after she realized she was pregnant and no one by the name he'd given her lived anywhere in Nevada."

"And there's a good chance Deidre didn't use the Walker name when she arranged to adopt me," Jessica added. "She told us that she knew Larissa was our father's mistress, but she said very little about her actual dealings with her. Just that she offered to adopt me and Larissa agreed."

"I don't suppose Larissa kept a journal of any kind," Sarah interjected sensibly. "Even copies of papers related to the adoption might give us a clue as to where to go next."

"I can't remember Larissa ever writing in a journal, but that doesn't mean she never did," Abby replied. "And I haven't had a chance to go through her personal papers yet. We could find something among them that might be helpful. If nothing turns up, we can also talk to Hank and Judith. They are definitely going to want to meet you—no matter what."

Feeling like she wanted to pinch herself to make sure all that had happened in the past hour or so was real, Abby stood and gestured toward the hallway that led to her mother's bedroom.

"I had planned to go through her things today. You're welcome to give me a hand if you want. With three of us looking for clues about our birth, we shouldn't miss anything."

"Are you sure you feel up to it right now?" Sarah asked solicitously. "We've dumped an awful lot on you all at once."

"The sooner the mystery is solved, the better…for all of us," Abby assured her as she led the way down the narrow hallway. "The bathroom is here, just in case you need it. There's raspberry iced tea in the refrigerator, too, in case you're ready for a cold drink."

"Maybe in a little while," Jessica said, revealing an eagerness to get started on the search that her sisters obviously shared.

At Abby's suggestion, the three of them went through all the drawers in the dresser, the chest and the nightstands, looking for a journal of any sort. Sarah and Jessica seemed a bit hesitant at first to handle their birth mother's things. Though they soon relaxed, some of their initial reverence lingered.

When they found nothing, Abby asked Jessica to take down the cardboard file box that held Larissa's personal papers from the closet shelf. Sitting in a circle on Larissa's bed, they spread out the contents, sorting through old bank statements, bills and receipts, and the various cards either Abby, her grandparents or one of Larissa's more thoughtful male friends had given her over the years.

Again, they found nothing helpful except for a copy of Abby's birth certificate. Abby hadn't really studied it closely for years. Eyeing it now, she remembered the first time she had looked at it. She had been waiting in line to apply for her first driver's license.

Almost seventeen at the time, she'd been older than most of her classmates when they had first gotten behind the wheel, but she'd had to save up to pay for her car insurance before Hank would teach her to drive.

Standing there, she had focused on the line where her father's name should have been written, her face burning a bright red as she stared at the single boldly typed word—*unknown*. Only her desperate desire to be able to get around town on her own in Hank's old truck had overcome her excruciating embarrassment at having to hand over the certificate to the clerk on duty.

Since then, she had made it a point never to actually peruse the document when, for whatever reason, she had to produce it.

Today, however, Abby studied it closely, line by line, along with Sarah and Jessica. And there she noticed for the first time that she hadn't been born in a hospital as she had always assumed.

She, and more than likely, her sisters, too, had been born at an address that could be a clinic, perhaps even a residence, somewhere in the Las Vegas area. And she hadn't been delivered by a doctor, as she'd also always assumed, but by a midwife named Henrietta Winslow.

"That's odd," Jessica murmured. "According to my birth certificate, I was born at Desert Valley Memorial Hospital in Las Vegas and I was delivered by a Dr. Robert Smith. The line for my birth mother's name has *unknown* typed in, and Lawrence Walker is listed as my father."

"And all I have are some papers from the hospital in Bellville stating the day and time when I was abandoned there, and the papers finalizing my adoption by Alice and Edward Daniels," Sarah said.

"There is no way we could have been born in separate places," Jessica stated pragmatically. "And how could my birth mother be unknown when Deidre knew enough about her to track her down twenty-seven years ago? I would lay odds that my birth certificate is a total fabrication except for my father's name. I can only begin to guess why. I'm sure Deidre must have been up to something. But what, exactly, Mother dearest?" she added with a hint of bitterness.

"What about my certificate, then?" Abby asked. "Do you think it's legitimate?"

"Probably so," Sarah said. "But there's only one way to find out for sure. We're going to have to track down the midwife, Henrietta Winslow, and ask her."

"If the Winslow woman delivered Abby, then she delivered all of us," Jessica pointed out. "Which means she might just be able to tell us what really happened that day."

"It's been a long time," Abby reminded them. "Mrs. Winslow could have moved out of state since then. She might even have passed away. And even if we are able to find her, there's a good chance she won't remember the exact circumstances of one delivery when she'd probably attended hundreds over the years."

"We have to at least try to find her, though," Sarah insisted. "Granted, Winslow is a fairly common name, but surely there is some sort of statewide listing of midwives. We know she was practicing in the Las Vegas area when we were born—"

The chiming of the doorbell cut off Sarah's eager words. Glancing at the clock on the nightstand, Abby saw that it was almost one o'clock, and she knew immediately who was at the front door.

"Help has arrived." Smiling at her sisters, Abby eased off the bed, her birth certificate in hand. As they eyed her questioningly, she gestured for them to come with her. "It's Jack," she explained, leading the way down the hall. "If anyone can find a midwife for us, it's him. He's a doctor. And my fiancé," she added shyly.

And he was about to get the surprise of his life, she thought to herself, hardly able to wait to see the look on his face when he realized there were three of her.

Well, sort of…

Chapter Twenty-One

The morning had gone by blessedly fast for Jack. There were several children in need of a physical for the various camps they would be attending during the coming summer months. Three patients were having problems with seasonal allergies, and one thirteen-year-old boy whose mother was sure his chest, back and face were covered with bug bites after a night of sleeping out in a tent in the backyard turned out to have a late case of chicken pox.

Focused as he had been on his work, Jack had still kept an eager eye on the clock, counting down the hours remaining before he could be with Abby again. He had thought about calling her to make sure she had seen his note, but he wouldn't have been able to talk to her nearly long enough. He would have ended up missing her more than ever, and that, in turn, would have been woefully distracting.

When noon had finally rolled around, and the last few people in the clinic's waiting room had been seen to, Jack finished dictating his notes, put the file folders on the secretary's desk, hung up his lab coat, and headed out the door with a wave of his hand to Edna.

He arrived at Abby's mother's house a few minutes later to find a car he didn't recognize parked at the curb out front. Probably someone interested in buying the house, he thought, disappointed that he and Abby would have to wait to pick up where they had left off that morning.

Standing on the little porch, waiting for Abby to answer the door, Jack hoped the people wouldn't be much longer. He had schooled himself to be patient most of the morning, but now he wanted nothing more than to have his fiancée all to himself so he could tell her—

The door swung open on a whoosh of air and Abby stood there, gazing up at him, a brilliant smile lighting up her face. As he smiled back, Jack realized that she was absolutely *glowing* with an inner excitement he had never seen her express before.

With her hair clipped back loosely enough to allow errant tendrils to frame her face, she looked utterly soft and feminine. But her eyes fairly sparkled and two bright spots of color rode high on her cheekbones, warning him that she could very well have some sort of mischief afoot.

"Hey..." he said for want of anything better as he reached out to touch her cheek.

"Hey, yourself." Without the slightest hesitation, she closed the distance between them and gave him a hug.

A rather perfunctory hug, though, considering how they had spent the night. Warm enough, and welcoming, but much too matter-of-fact and over much too soon for Jack's taste.

He had assumed, mistakenly it seemed, that *he* had been the one responsible for the radiance she exuded. But something else, or *someone* else, he thought, remembering the car parked at the curb, had done it.

Suffering an unaccustomed pang of jealousy, Jack let Abby take him by the hand and pull him into the house.

"You will never believe what happened this morning," she said, pausing to close the door. "In the space of a few hours, my whole life has been turned upside down."

In a good way, Jack assumed, considering the lilt in her voice. But by whom? Again, he experienced a moment's ill will toward the person or persons responsible for supplanting him in Abby's affections. Though that was probably going a bit overboard.

She seemed so sure he would share in her exhilaration. Certainly that would eliminate the possibility of it being another man—

Just a few steps into the living room, Jack halted in mid-stride as his gaze settled on the two women standing together by the sofa, identically tentative smiles curving their lips. Stunned, he drew a sharp breath, hardly able to believe his eyes.

How could two women who looked almost exactly like Abby be standing there so complacently? It had to be impossible, and yet, there they were—with the same auburn hair and bright blue eyes, the same height and the same build.

"What in the world...?" he muttered, barely resisting the urge to give his head a good shake in the hope of clearing his vision.

"That is exactly what I wondered when I opened the door this morning and saw them standing on the porch," Abby said, giving his hand a reassuring squeeze as she drew him farther into the living room.

Too confounded to put the half dozen questions he had into words, Jack looked down at Abby, willing her to explain.

"Come and meet my sisters." She gestured first to the woman with the shorter, curlier auburn hair, then to the one with the longer, wavy hair. "Sarah Daniels and Jessica Walker." Smiling, she looked up at him again. "And this is my fiancé, Jack Randall."

"Hi, Jack," Sarah said.

"Yes, hello," Jessica added.

Both offered their hands for him to shake, which he somehow managed to do as he nodded to one, then the other. He hated to admit it, but he was more confused than ever.

"Sisters…?" he asked, glancing at Abby again. Not just sisters, but identical triplets, he realized. "But how—?"

"It's a long story," Abby replied. "Maybe we had better sit down."

She motioned for Sarah and Jessica to take the sofa, then drew Jack over to the chair and ottoman. At her direction, he took the chair while she perched on the ottoman close by.

"We're not exactly sure how, but it seems we were separated right after we were born. Sarah and Jessica only found out about each other a few weeks ago, and they didn't know about me until today.

"They came to Promise to learn whatever they

could about Larissa. They knew she was their birth mother, but they had been told she was dead by Jessica's adoptive mother, and they were curious about her.

"We've spent the morning trying to figure out what happened all those years ago. How we were separated the way we were, and why."

As Jack listened in astonished silence, the three women repeated the information they had exchanged prior to his arrival. Sarah explained how she had been mistaken for Jessica, and Jessica explained how she and Sarah had thought they were twins, only to discover that they were actually triplets.

By the time they finished their recitation, Jack was just as puzzled as they obviously were about Larissa Summers' actions. That Jessica, alone, had been raised as part of their birth father's family also seemed odd to him.

He had heard of the Nevada real estate mogul, Stuart Walker. Surely, a man of his wealth and prestige would have welcomed not only his three infant granddaughters into his home, but their birth mother, too, under the circumstances. He thought it was equally strange that while Deidre Walker had been able to track down Larissa so she could adopt Lawrence Walker's child, she also claimed to have had no knowledge of Sarah, or by extension, Abby, either. And when Sarah and Jessica had professed to have an interest in meeting their birth mother, Deidre had known, as well, that she was dead.

To Jack, something about what the woman knew and claimed not to know just didn't jibe. When he pointed that out to Abby and her sisters, they all nodded in agreement.

"We looked through Larissa's personal papers, hoping to find some clue as to what really happened when we were born," Abby explained. "All we found was a copy of my birth certificate. That left us with even more questions since it lists different details than Jessica's birth certificate does."

Abby took the folded document from the pocket of her jumper and handed it to Jack. As he looked at it, she continued.

"We thought if we could find the midwife who delivered me, maybe she could fill in some of the blanks for us. But we're not sure exactly how to go about it."

"I could do some research on the computer at the clinic," Jack offered, as anxious as Abby and her sisters were to solve the mystery surrounding their birth and separation. "Since we're closed for the day, we would be the only ones there, so you can come along, too, if you'd like."

"Oh, yes," Abby, Sarah and Jessica agreed in unison.

Then Abby's stomach let out a ferocious growl, and she groaned as the others laughed.

"Sorry about that," she muttered, her face red.

"No problem," Jack assured her, taking her by the hand and pulling her to her feet. "We'll stop and grab some burgers on the way to the clinic, then you three can eat while I surf the Net."

Finding the midwife who had delivered Abby turned out to take much less time than Jack had anticipated. Though she must have been at, or beyond, retirement age, Henrietta Winslow was still listed in the state's directory of licensed and certified nurse/midwives, and the address given for her was the same as the one written down as the place of birth on Abby's birth certificate.

A telephone number was given, as well, and Jack offered to make the initial call since he could truthfully tell whoever answered that he was a doctor looking for a midwife.

With Abby, Sarah and Jessica sitting around him in his office, watching him with eager expectation, he dialed the number. After three rings, he was greeted by a woman's harried-sounding voice. Jack gave his name and asked for Henrietta.

"Henrietta is my mother-in-law," the woman replied. "She's retired now and living in a nursing home." After a pause, during which Jack heard her yelling at someone named Bert, she came back on the line and added, "She'd been having a lot of health problems lately and I just couldn't cope with her here."

Jack expressed his regrets, then asked if the woman would mind giving him the name of the nursing home where Henrietta now resided.

The woman hesitated, then asked suspiciously, "Why do you want to know that? Did you used to work with her or something?"

"Years ago," Jack answered, hoping he would be forgiven such a bald-faced lie since his intentions were good.

"Oh, well, okay then. She's in the Golden Meadows Nursing Home on Apricot Lane, about fifteen miles east of downtown Vegas."

The woman gave Jack the home's telephone number, as well, and he wrote it down along with the name and address. Then he thanked her and said goodbye.

Three pairs of bright blue eyes fixed on him as he looked up from the pad of paper he'd been using.

"You found her?" Abby asked.

"Yes, I found her," Jack replied, holding up the piece of paper on which he'd written the pertinent information.

"Can we go to see her now?" Jessica stood and slipped her purse strap over her shoulder, obviously ready.

"She's in a nursing home on the east side of Las Vegas, about an hour and a half drive from here." Jack glanced at Abby. Along with Sarah, she, too, was standing now. "Are you sure you're up to it?"

"Oh, yes," Abby assured him. "I'm fine now that I've eaten. And I don't think any of us could stand the anticipation of waiting until tomorrow or the next day."

"All right, then. I'll take you," Jack said.

"Thank you, thank you, *thank you*," Abby cried as she came around the side of his desk to give him a hug that was anything but perfunctory.

Jack held her close as long as she let him, relieved that she was willing to include him in what might prove to be a very traumatic encounter for her and her sisters.

He wouldn't have allowed them to make the trip alone under any circumstances. But he had been afraid Abby might refuse his offer out of a misguided sense of pride.

She had to know, as did Sarah and Jessica, that at least some of what the midwife could tell them might not be too good. He didn't want any of them to have to deal with whatever secrets of the past the woman chose to reveal on their own, most especially Abby.

She had overcome so much alone already. Jack wanted her to know that as long as he could draw breath, she would never have to face another demon on her own again.

Though with Sarah and Jessica a part of her life now, maybe she wouldn't really need him any-more—

Shoving that particularly disheartening thought out of his mind—at least for the time being—Jack locked up the clinic, settled Abby and her sisters in his car, and headed for the highway leading out of Promise.

As the miles spun away, Abby, Sarah and Jessica sat quietly, hardly saying a word. Jack could only imagine what they were thinking. And he hoped against hope that by day's end they wouldn't be sorry they had set out on this journey into their past.

Chapter Twenty-Two

Abby was more grateful than she could say that Jack had offered to take her and her sisters to see Henrietta Winslow. Sitting on the passenger seat of his car, she spent most of the nearly two-hour drive gazing out the window at the rather bland scenery.

In the back seat, Sarah and Jessica sat together, poring over the two photograph albums containing pictures of Larissa, Hank and Judith, and herself as a child growing up in Promise that she had dug out of a box for them before they'd left for the clinic.

Jessica had shown her the old photograph of their father and the more recent one of their grandfather that she carried in her wallet, providing faces for the names of the family Abby had never known she had.

Abby had seen at once why Larissa had fallen in love with Lawrence Walker. He had been a handsome man with a humorous glint in his eyes all those years ago. He hadn't looked like the type who would totally abandon a woman pregnant with his child even though he'd been married. And maybe he wouldn't have if he hadn't died in a plane crash.

From what Jessica and Sarah had said about Stuart Walker, he didn't seem like the kind of man who would have abandoned two of his three granddaughters, along with their mother, either. Obviously, he hadn't known about them. But someone had—the same someone who had arranged for Deidre Walker to adopt her dead husband's daughter, Jessica.

Why hadn't that person told Deidre about her and Sarah? And why had their father's true identity been kept a secret from Larissa?

By the time they reached the nursing home on the outskirts of Las Vegas, Abby's head was spinning with unanswered questions. From the solemn looks on Sarah and Jessica's faces, they, too, had become more and more puzzled by what had, and *hadn't,* happened almost twenty-seven years ago.

"Do you want me to come inside with you?" Jack asked as he pulled into a parking place and shut off the car's engine.

"Yes, please," Abby replied, shooting him an appreciative glance.

Holding on to his hand for moral support, she led the way with him to the home's double glass front doors, Sarah and Jessica following along behind them.

The long, low, one-story brick building set on a small patch of lawn with neatly trimmed shrubs dotted here and there looked nice enough. Inside, it was cool and clean and quiet. The woman sitting at the reception desk looked up from the magazine she was reading and greeted them with a welcoming smile.

"May I help you?" she asked, her eyes widening as she noted the striking resemblance of the three young women.

"We've come to visit Mrs. Henrietta Winslow," Jack said.

He introduced himself as Dr. Jack Randall, then added that he had spoken to Mrs. Winslow's daughter-in-law earlier in the afternoon and she had approved of their visiting her mother-in-law.

"Oh, yes, no problem," the receptionist replied. "We encourage family and friends to visit as often as possible. It really helps to keep everyone's spirits up. Let me make sure Mrs. Winslow is in her room."

A quick call to the nurse on duty confirmed that Mrs. Winslow was in her room. She was also up to seeing her visitors, but only for half an hour or so since she had been a bit under the weather the past few days.

"Her room is through that doorway and down the corridor," the receptionist advised, gesturing to her right. "Room 115 on the right side of the hallway."

"I can wait for you here if you'd like to talk to Mrs. Winslow on your own," Jack said as they started toward the doorway.

Abby didn't mind having Jack along. In fact, she wanted him with her just in case Mrs. Winslow couldn't answer their questions. But she had her sisters' feelings to consider, as well. She looked at them questioningly, and to her relief, they smiled and said in unison, "No, please, come with us," then laughed along with Abby and Jack.

Together, they walked down the corridor to Mrs.

Winslow's room, and paused on the threshold to knock tentatively, announcing their presence.

"Come in," a querulous voice instructed them.

As they entered the large, brightly sunlit room, Abby's gaze was drawn to the elderly woman sitting in a wheelchair by the window. Her close-cropped hair was iron gray, her face lined with age, her mouth downturned in permanent dissatisfaction. But her hazel eyes were sharp and clear, and wearing a pretty pink robe, she looked much sturdier than Abby had anticipated.

"And who are you?" Mrs. Winslow demanded, her frown deepening as she looked at Abby.

A moment later, though, her mouth opened in an O and her eyes widened with surprise as her gaze slid past Abby to Sarah and Jessica.

"I'm Abby Summers, Mrs. Winslow," Abby said, moving farther into the room. "And these are my sisters, Sarah Daniels and Jessica Walker."

The three stood in a semicircle with Abby, in the middle, as their spokeswoman, while Jack stayed near the doorway, hands in his pockets, taking a back seat to the proceedings, yet seeming ready to step in, if necessary, to help in any way he could.

"Summers, you say?" Mrs. Winslow sat back in her chair and nervously licked her lips.

Again, her gaze shifted to Sarah, then Jessica, before settling on Abby once more. Though she didn't admit it, she seemed to recognize the name.

"My mother—*our* mother—was Larissa Summers."

"I see," Mrs. Winslow murmured, her tone still noncommittal.

"Your name was listed on my birth certificate as

the midwife who delivered me almost twenty-seven years ago,'' Abby continued. ''I was born at the house where your daughter-in-law now lives. I believe my sisters were also born there and that you delivered them, as well. And I think that you might know how and why Sarah and Jessica were separated from our mother.''

For several long moments, Henrietta Winslow stared silently at Abby, making her wonder if the woman knew anything beyond the fact that she had delivered them. Or maybe she knew more, but was afraid to admit it because she had been involved in something illegal.

''We're not here to cause you any trouble, Mrs. Winslow,'' Jessica said kindly, her thoughts obviously running parallel to Abby's.

''What's done is done,'' Sarah added. ''But we're hoping that by knowing why we were separated we'll be able to make peace with the past.''

Mrs. Winslow hesitated a few seconds longer, then nodded her head once, her mind obviously made up.

''You're right. I did deliver all three of you, and a difficult delivery it was. A woman by the name of Cecelia Winthrop came to me with your mother. Said she was expecting twins. Also said she would pay me handsomely to handle the delivery and keep quiet about it. I had kids of my own and I needed the money, so I agreed.

''Apparently, the Winthrop woman had made some kind of financial deal with the Summers woman, too. As I understood it, she was supposed to take one of the babies for herself and leave the other for Miss Summers. Seemed to have a lot of money, that Winthrop woman, and she wanted a baby, but on the quiet, you know? Didn't want the babies born in a hospital. She had her own lawyer lined up to make it all legal, too.

"As it turned out, the birth was more involved than I anticipated because there were three of you instead of the two we were expecting. Poor Miss Summers passed out toward the end so she never knew about the third baby. The Winthrop woman insisted we keep it a secret, and she paid me extra not to say anything. She took two of you with her when she left, and I figured it was just as well—two of you growing up in a wealthy home and all.

"I'm not proud of what I did. Hiding the third baby from Miss Summers was wrong. I admit that. But I really needed the money back then..."

Abby stared at Mrs. Winslow, too stunned by her revelations to speak. Beside her, Jessica drew an audible breath.

"This Mrs. Winthrop," she began, her voice quavering. "Can you...can you tell me what she looked like?"

"A short little thing, blond hair, lots of makeup and jewelry. Not really pretty, but she knew how to make the most of what she had," Mrs. Winslow replied.

Jessica rustled around in her purse, pulled out her wallet and slipped a photograph from it.

"Is this the woman you knew as Cecelia Winthrop?" she asked.

Henrietta Winslow took the photograph Jessica offered her and studied it closely, then looked up at Jessica, obviously puzzled.

"Why, yes, that's her," she said. "She looks older

here.'' She tapped the photograph with her finger. ''Even so, I recognize her.''

''Deidre...'' Jessica murmured, sounding betrayed. ''Deidre knew about all three of us from the very beginning, but she kept it a secret. She had a hand in separating us, too. And she had Grandfather believing all these years that I was the sole surviving offspring of his only son.''

''She must have taken me with her, too, Jessica,'' Sarah said. ''But then, I got sick...''

''And Deidre wouldn't have wanted to risk explaining how she came to have two newborn babies, one of them seriously ill, to hospital personnel, so she just left you there and took me home to Willow Springs,'' Jessica added.

''And Larissa took me home to Promise thinking she had done the best she could for each of her *two* daughters,'' Abby said. ''Even if she had known our father's real name, with Deidre posing as Cecelia Winthrop, she would have never known that the woman so eager to adopt one of her babies was his wife, and still a part of his wealthy family.''

''What a mess.'' Jessica took the photograph from Mrs. Winslow and angrily shoved it back in her wallet. ''And all instigated by my mother, who no doubt was more interested in maintaining her status within the Walker family than anything else.

''If she had really cared about our father and our grandfather, and if she had really cared about me— about *us*—she would have told Stuart the truth about Larissa's relationship with Lawrence and the *three* granddaughters she had borne for him.''

Abby didn't know what to say to Jessica, and neither, it seemed, did Sarah. Each put an arm around her, though, offering what comfort they could, aware that she was angry on *their* behalf as well as her own.

"Thank you for being so honest, Mrs. Winslow." Jack stepped forward as he spoke to the old woman, who looked as if she'd had a weight lifted from her shoulders.

"I should have spoken up sooner, but I was too afraid," Mrs. Winslow allowed. "And anyway, who would I have told? Cecelia Winthrop wasn't even a real person. And poor Miss Summers—what could she have done?"

Abby turned to Jack gratefully, as did Sarah and Jessica. He reached out and enveloped them all in a reassuring hug, then stood back and touched Abby on the cheek.

"Let's head back to Promise, okay? We can decide what to do next on the way home."

The three sisters thanked Henrietta Winslow, then followed Jack's lead back to the car, chattering as they went.

"I know what I'm going to do," Jessica stated in a determined tone. "I'm going to call Grandfather and have a long talk with him just as soon as we get back to Promise."

"Maybe we ought to just go back to Willow Springs. All of us," Sarah said, including Abby with a slight smile. "Then we can tell him, and Deidre, all that we've found out."

"We should go to see Hank and Judith first though," Abby interjected.

"Oh, yes, we should do that first," Jessica agreed.

"Then we'll go to Willow Springs and talk to Stuart,'' Sarah said. ''He'll know best how to deal with Deidre.''

''He most certainly will,'' Jessica muttered, her tight smile not nearly enough to hide the pain she had to be feeling at her adoptive mother's betrayal.

Chapter Twenty-Three

During the drive back to Promise, Abby, Sarah and Jessica agreed on a plan of action based on what Henrietta Winslow had told them about their birth and subsequent separation. The next day, Sunday, Abby would take her sisters to meet Hank and Judith. Then, together, the three of them would head for Willow Springs to confront Deidre in front of their grandfather, Stuart.

The woman had obviously taken terrible advantage of Larissa, keeping her in the dark about the Walker family while offering her money she must have desperately needed to give up one of her babies for adoption. Deidre had been equally unfair to Stuart, too, hiding from him the fact that he actually had three granddaughters instead of just one.

Had Deidre been an honest, decent person, Larissa would have been able to raise all three of her children without having to struggle, and Abby, Sarah and Jessica would have grown up together as they should have.

Abby felt especially sorry for Jessica. Finding out that the woman who had raised her was a liar and a cheat had been very hard on her.

And, of course, Larissa hadn't been totally blameless herself. No one had forced her to go along with Deidre Walker. Which could explain why she had never been truly happy. Larissa might have told herself that she'd had no choice about giving away one of her babies, but she must have always known, deep in her heart, that she had.

With a sigh, Abby looked out the window as they entered the outskirts of Promise. They had been driving along in silence for the past thirty minutes or so, each of them caught up in their own thoughts.

Beside her, Jack reached across the console and took her hand in his, giving it a gentle, reassuring squeeze. Looking over at him, Abby smiled gratefully.

"Thanks," she said.

"For what?" he asked, arching an eyebrow as he glanced at her.

"For smoothing the way for us with Mrs. Winslow. For giving us all a strong shoulder to lean on." Though she continued to cling to his hand as if it were a lifeline, she lowered her gaze. "For just…being here."

"There's nowhere else I'd rather be, Abby, than here with you," he assured her.

Jack drove through downtown Promise, then turned onto the street that led to her mother's house. As they drew closer, Abby saw that Jessica's rental car was still parked at the curb. But there was also a larger, more luxurious car, a limousine actually, parked behind it.

"Looks like you have another visitor," Jack observed, slowing to pull into the driveway.

"Mother—" Jessica said, apparently recognizing the car, anger riding over the surprise in her voice.

"Come to do a little damage control, I imagine," Sarah added, her tone matter-of-fact. "Considering how fast on her feet she was when I showed up in Willow Springs with Ryan, we should have known she wouldn't waste any time heading for Promise once she found out we were here."

"I wonder what she planned to say to us about Abby and Larissa," Jessica mused. "How she thought she could carry on her deception..."

"She could have gone on claiming ignorance of my existence as well as Sarah's," Abby said. "We wouldn't have known any different if we hadn't talked to Henrietta Winslow."

"I doubt she considered the possibility that we would find her," Jessica added. "But we did."

As Jack turned off the car's engine, the limousine driver stepped out and opened one of the rear doors. A moment later, Abby saw a petite blond woman emerge.

Though she was elegantly dressed in a knee-length, tailored white linen skirt and a flattering, royal-blue, short-sleeved sweater, and decked out in enough gold-and-diamond jewelry to fund a small army, there was a distinctly frazzled look about her.

Her silvery-gold hair wasn't quite as neatly styled as Abby imagined it usually was, and her makeup appeared to be less than expertly applied.

"Do you want me to run interference for you?" Jack asked as Abby and her sisters sat in the car. "I can get rid of her, at least for awhile. That would give you time to sort out what you want to say to her."

"I don't know about Abby and Sarah, but I'd just as soon deal with her now," Jessica replied.

Abby and Sarah murmured in agreement. Since Jessica would be taking the lead, and she seemed more than ready for the coming showdown, all they would really have to do was lend their support.

"You'll stay close, though, won't you, Jack?" Abby asked. "Just in case…"

"Wild horses couldn't drag me away," he vowed with a grin. "Okay, ladies, ready?"

"Ready," they answered in unison

As Abby, Sarah and Jessica, along with Jack, climbed out of the car, Deidre skidded to a halt on the sidewalk.

"Oh, my goodness," she called out in a syrupy voice. "Don't tell me you have *another* sister, Jessica, darling."

"All right, Mother, I won't," Jessica replied, her own voice tightly controlled.

"But, sweetie, you can't think that I *knew*—"

Taking Deidre by the arm, Jessica cut in brusquely, "I think we'd better go inside, Mother. Then you can tell us all about what you knew and didn't know twenty-seven years ago. Unless Abby and Sarah have any objections."

"None at all," Sarah said.

"No, not a one," Abby agreed, slipping her key into the lock and opening the door.

Inside, Deidre broke free of Jessica's hold on her

arm and strode into the living room, arms spread wide.

"Well, isn't this...quaint," she cooed, offering Abby a smile that didn't quite hide the panic glittering in her eyes. "This is where you grew up...Abby?"

"Yes," Abby answered her, somewhat unnerved by the woman.

She had the kind of mow-you-over, my-way-or-the-highway personality that Abby had always found extremely intimidating.

Sarah, who had had a taste of Deidre Walker's forcefulness already, seemed quietly amused by the woman's posturing. And Jessica, who had grown up under Deidre's domineering thumb, made no effort to hide her outrage at the woman's continuing attempt at deception as she squared off with her.

"Sit down, Mother," she said, pointing to the chair, her tone brooking no argument.

"Now, Jessica, *darling,* there's no need—"

"We went to see Henrietta Winslow this afternoon," Jessica continued as if Deidre hadn't spoken. "You remember her, don't you? She's the midwife who delivered us."

Deidre stared at Jessica in silence, unable to hide her horror as she sank slowly onto the edge of the chair cushion. After a moment, she blinked her eyes and looked away. Folding her hands primly in her lap, she tipped her pointed chin at a defiant angle.

"I'm sure I don't know who you're talking about, sweetie. As I've already told both you and Sarah, I thought Lawrence's mistress had only one baby, the baby I adopted—*you,* Jessica."

"But you were there when we were born, Mother,

posing as Cecelia Winthrop. Mrs. Winslow identified you from the photograph I have in my wallet,'' Jessica said. Hands on her hips, she stood facing Deidre, with Abby and Sarah on either side of her. ''You didn't adopt me through some nameless intermediary as you've always said. You met with Larissa Summers face-to-face and struck a deal with her. And when three babies were born instead of the two you were expecting, it was your idea to keep Larissa in the dark about it. You took two of us for yourself, instead, but when Sarah got sick, you abandoned her at a hospital like so much unwanted baggage.''

Seeming to realize that she had been irrefutably found out, Deidre lifted her hands to her chest in a fluttery motion.

''Nothing went the way I'd planned,'' she whined piteously, though Abby saw the sly glimmer in her eyes. ''I thought I was doing the Summers woman a favor, taking two of her brats—uh, babies—off her hands. Then you started having trouble breathing.'' She shot a reproachful look Sarah's way. ''I had to dump you or I would have been in big trouble.'' Deidre shifted her gaze back to Jessica. ''Just *think* of the kind of life you would have had *then,* darling. I just wanted the best for you—''

''Too bad you didn't want the best for all of us,'' Jessica retorted. ''Especially when you could have gotten it for us simply by telling Grandfather about Larissa in the first place. He would have taken care of her and of us, too.''

''Oh, but I couldn't do that,'' Deidre replied with a dismissive flutter of her bejeweled fingers. ''Stuart would have had that horrible, lowlife woman living in *my* house, taking *my* place in the Walker family.''

Abby felt a searing wave of pain wash over her at Deidre's cruel comment. An instant later, Jack came up beside her and slipped his arm around her shoulders. She leaned against him, thankful for his support and understanding.

"You're talking about our birth mother," Jessica reminded Deidre in an icy voice. "And the house in Willow Springs isn't yours, it's Grandfather's. As for your place there, it's going to be nonexistent once we tell Stuart what you've done."

"Oh, no, you can't do that. You can't, you can't, you *can't*." Her voice rising to a piercing shriek, Deidre leapt to her feet and went after Jessica, her hands curled into claws, her eyes flashing maniacally.

Only Jack's quick reflexes prevented her from gouging Jessica's face with her long, ruby-red nails.

Deidre struggled with Jack for several seconds, but even in her agitated state, she was no match for him. At his instruction, Abby went out to the car to retrieve his medical bag. By the time she returned, Deidre was sitting on the chair again, arms clasped around her middle, rocking back and forth, muttering to herself incoherently.

"I don't think I'm going to have to give her a sedative, after all," Jack said. "I've called an ambulance, though. She's going to need to be hospitalized, at least temporarily."

"It's my fault," Jessica murmured, her remorse evident in her voice.

"She had to be told that we knew the truth," Sarah stated pragmatically, leading Jessica to the sofa and sitting down with her. "The way she was behaving, there was no nice way to do it."

''Our lives could have been so different if she had been a different kind of person,'' Abby added, standing close beside Jack as he kept a professional eye on Deidre.

''You're both right, of course,'' Jessica agreed.

When the ambulance arrived a few minutes later, Jack saw to it that Deidre was handled gently. He also rode along to the hospital with her to spare Jessica that unfortunate task, promising to make sure she received the best care available.

Abby offered to let Jessica and Sarah use her mother's room, but both women insisted on returning to their motel for the night.

Jessica wanted to call their grandfather and apprise him of the situation with Deidre, as well as her discovery of a third sister in Promise, Nevada. She also wanted to talk to her fiancé, Sam, and Sarah, too, was eager to get in touch with her fiancé, Ryan.

After agreeing to meet at the house the next morning, they exchanged hugs and said goodbye. Stopping only to send Deidre's driver back to Willow Springs, Jessica and Sarah left in Jessica's rental car, and Abby went inside the house again, relieved to be on her own, after all. Considering the day they'd had, she needed some time to herself, and obviously, Jessica and Sarah had felt the same way.

Alone in the quiet house, Abby curled up on the sofa, mentally sifting through all she had learned that day about Larissa and herself, about her sisters and the Walker family, and about Jack—dear, sweet, wonderful Jack, who had stood by her so staunchly.

In the flurry of loading Deidre into the ambulance, he hadn't had a chance to say if he would come back that night. Keeping in mind all that *he* had been through, Abby didn't really expect him to. In fact, he probably needed some quiet time of his own.

But it would be so nice if he did return, even for a little while, she thought, smiling as she closed her eyes and drifted off to sleep.

Chapter Twenty-Four

Jack had decided that if Sarah and Jessica were still with Abby when he finished checking Deidre into the hospital, he would go on home to his apartment. But when he pulled up to her mother's house just after eight-thirty, their rental car was no longer parked at the curb.

The house itself looked dark and deserted, as if Abby might not be there, either. She could be with her sisters, perhaps finishing a late dinner. Or she could be with her grandparents, filling them in on all she had learned about her mother, her sisters, and her ties to the Walker family.

Jack suspected she was actually at home, though, dealing with the events of the day on her own, trying to make sense of all that had happened, past and present, and considering how it would affect her future.

Abby had a whole new family now—sisters to share her joys and sorrows, and a very, very wealthy grandfather who would surely be eager to make up for lost time with his newfound granddaughter.

Jack was really happy about Abby's sudden, unexpected good fortune. At the same time, though, he couldn't help but be afraid that somehow he would be edged out of her life. Granted, she had leaned on him during the worst of the ordeal she had gone through with Henrietta Winslow and Deidre Walker. But his had been the only strong shoulder available.

That wouldn't be the case once Stuart Walker arrived on the scene. He could easily sweep Abby off into a whirl of excitement that wouldn't necessarily include a small-town pediatrician, no matter how much the pediatrician loved her.

Jack didn't want to keep Abby from having all the wonderful experiences Stuart Walker would want to provide for her. But he didn't want to lose her, either.

He hadn't had a chance to tell her how much he loved her during the long afternoon and early evening they had spent with Sarah and Jessica. And now, with everything else that had occurred, he wasn't sure he should—at least not just yet.

He couldn't just drive away, though. Not without checking to see if she was at home.

Jack parked his car in the driveway and walked to the front door, trying not to get his hopes up. He rang the bell and waited; glanced at his watch and rang the bell one more time. He was about to turn away when, to his vast relief, the porch light came on and the door opened slowly.

Abby peered out at him through bleary eyes, her loose ponytail coming undone, her T-shirt and denim jumper rumpled. In an instant, her expression brightened. Smiling, she reached out for him.

"Oh, Jack, I was hoping you would come back," she said as she stepped into his embrace.

He hugged her hard against him, then kissed the top of her head.

"But I woke you up."

"Good thing, too. I dozed off on the sofa. Much longer on those lumpy cushions and I would have been too stiff and sore to stand up." She took a step back and looked up at him. "Can you stay?"

"Until you put me out," he assured her with a grin.

"Not a chance of that tonight." She smiled, too, with more than a hint of flirtation, then took him by the hand and led him into the house.

Jack had just closed the door when Abby's stomach growled, making her giggle.

"Have you eaten since lunch?" he asked, frowning down at her.

"No," she admitted. "So much was going on that I forgot. Then everyone left, and I was so tired that I fell asleep on the sofa." She reached up and unfastened what was left of her ponytail. "Now what I want even more than food is a long, hot shower."

"Go have one while I rustle up something for us to eat."

"Oh, thank you," she murmured as she stretched tall to give him a kiss on the cheek. "That would be lovely."

"My pleasure," he replied, cupping her face in his hand and feathering a light kiss of his own on her lips.

At least he had meant it to be a light kiss. Once

in progress, it quickly deepened into something that had him wanting to follow her into the shower as he had done the night before. Only his promise to fix her a meal had him turning toward the kitchen as she headed down the hallway.

Jack found a large container of homemade vegetable soup labeled with her grandmother's handwriting in the refrigerator and a package of yeast rolls in the freezer. By the time Abby joined him, looking somewhat refreshed in her short, sexy, royal blue silk robe, he had the table set, the soup pot bubbling and the rolls ready to come out of the oven.

"Mmm, smells wonderful," Abby said as she slid onto a chair by the table.

"All compliments of your grandmother, I believe," Jack replied as he ladled soup into their bowls.

"She's been spoiling me with all of her cooking and baking."

After Jack joined her at the table, they ate in silence for a few minutes. Then Abby asked him about Deidre.

"For the time being, she'll be under the care of our staff psychiatrist at the hospital here in Promise," Jack explained. "But it's more than likely that she's going to need long-term care which I'm sure Jessica and Stuart will want to arrange for her in the Willow Springs area."

"Will she be all right?"

"Physically, yes, but I'm not really sure about her mental well-being. She went into a catatonic state this evening. Whether she ever comes out of it is anybody's guess. She's done some terrible things, and she may never be able to face the repercussions.''

''In a way, that was true of my mother, too,'' Abby admitted sadly. ''She spent all the years since she gave birth to me and my sisters running away from what she had done in one way or another. All of our lives could have been so different if she and Deidre had made other choices.''

''For what it's worth, I don't think either one of them meant you, Sarah or Jessica any harm,'' Jack said, reaching across the table to cover her hand with his.

''I don't think so, either.'' With a weary smile, Abby pushed her empty bowl away, then added, ''And we've found each other, at last. That, alone, makes up for a lot.''

''I would say it does, too,'' Jack agreed, eyeing Abby closely from across the table. ''I'd also say it's time I tucked you into bed. You look beat.''

''Let me help with the dishes, first,'' she protested, though only halfheartedly.

''I'll take care of the cleanup.'' He came around the table, took her by the hand and pulled her to her feet.

Abby went along with him willingly, yawning hugely as they walked down the hallway to her bedroom. She had left the lamp on the nightstand lit, and in its warm glow she looked lovelier than ever to Jack.

She slipped out of her robe unselfconsciously, and slid, naked, under the bedcovers. Scooting over to the wall, she patted the narrow space beside her.

''Stay with me awhile?'' she asked, her gaze holding his.

"Until you put me out," he answered her as he'd done earlier.

"Not a chance of that tonight," she, too, repeated.

Jack took only a few moments to shed his clothes—consigning the dinner dishes to a morning scrubbing. Then he lay down beside Abby and turned off the lamp.

She snuggled close to him, deliciously warm, the faint scent of her lavender soap clinging to her delicate skin, and yawned again.

"Sorry," she said, laughing softly.

"Don't be."

He gently turned her so she faced away from him, then curved his body around hers, spoon-style, one hand cupping her belly, the other cradling her breast.

"Just sleep," he murmured against her hair.

She put a hand over his and sighed quietly as she relaxed against him.

"You, too."

"Yes," Jack assured her. "Me, too."

But he didn't—not for a long time, at least. He stared into the darkness, dreading the days ahead when Abby would be swept up, and perhaps away, by her new family.

Would the love he had to offer her—the love she had yet to even believe in—be enough to make her stay with him in Promise? Or would he be offering her too little, too late?

He knew he was going to find out very soon, whether he wanted to or not...

Chapter Twenty-Five

Abby awoke early Sunday morning to the distant sound of the telephone ringing. Despite the dozing she had done on the sofa earlier in the evening, she had slept straight through the night. And even though she was now awake, she was feeling too groggy to jump up and run to the kitchen to answer the phone.

Beside her, Jack shifted, swinging his legs over the edge of the bed.

"I'll get it," he said as he grabbed his slacks and started toward the doorway.

Abby rolled onto her side and watched him go with a pang of regret. They had finally awakened in bed together, but thanks to the ringing telephone, they hadn't had a chance to savor the moment as she would have liked.

Liked very much, indeed, she amended, smiling

with pleasure as she caught a last glimpse of Jack's broad, bare back, tight butt and muscular thighs.

Aware that she would probably have to speak to whoever was calling, Abby sat up reluctantly and reached for her robe. She had it on, with the belt tied, and was sitting on the side of the bed, trying to blink away the last of her sleepiness when Jack came back into the bedroom.

"It's Jessica," he said. "She wanted to let you know that your grandfather, along with her fiancé and Sarah's, are on their way to Promise. They should be here by ten. She said that she and Sarah would be here at eight-thirty. Then the three of you will have time to see Hank and Judith first, so you can explain everything to them. As long as that's okay with you."

"Oh, yes, that's okay with me," Abby replied, glancing at the clock.

She had an hour to get ready—more than enough time under normal circumstances. But she was going to be meeting Stuart Walker today—something she hadn't expected to be doing quite so soon.

"I'll tell her, then." Jack turned to go back to the kitchen, then glanced at Abby, again. "Do you want me to let your grandparents know we'll be coming over, or would you rather call them yourself?"

Abby knew she should make the call, but she also knew Jack would be much more casual about their early Sunday morning visit. She didn't want Hank and Judith to be alarmed for no reason, and she would have a hard time hiding her own nervousness.

"Are you sure you don't mind calling them for me?" she asked.

"Not at all. You go get ready."

''Their telephone number is on the—''

''Pad by the telephone,'' he finished for her. ''I'll call them, then I'm going to head over to my place and change clothes. I'll be back here by eight-thirty, though.''

Abby hopped off the bed and ran to him.

''Thanks,'' she said, raising up to kiss his cheek. ''For everything.''

Jack pulled her hard against his chest and gave her a long, slow, utterly delicious kiss on the mouth.

''You're very welcome,'' he murmured as he released her. ''Now get going. And don't forget to eat something.''

''Not likely,'' she assured him, patting her tummy with a grin.

The rest of the day passed in a mind-boggling whirlwind of activity, starting with the drive to Hank and Judith's apartment and Abby's introduction of Sarah and Jessica to their grandparents. After the first long moments of stunned disbelief, Hank and Judith welcomed Abby's sisters with hugs and kisses and tears of wonder and joy.

With Jack sitting quietly off to one side, his mere presence offering Abby a full measure of much-needed support, she, along with Sarah and Jessica, revealed all that they now knew about how and why they had been separated, as well as how they had come to find each other at last.

Hank and Judith took in all they were told as best they could. But Abby knew it would be awhile before they fully understood all that had occurred almost twenty-seven years ago, not to mention all that was happening that very day.

One thing was certain, though. They were thrilled

to find out they had three granddaughters, and that, more than anything, seemed to make up for any pain they might have felt as a result of the unfortunate choices Larissa had once made.

Since Jessica had given Stuart directions to Larissa's house, they headed back there, along with Hank and Judith, shortly before ten o'clock.

Having flown from Willow Springs to Las Vegas in a private jet, Stuart, Ryan Noble and Sam Dawson completed their journey to Promise in a chauffeur-driven limousine.

When Abby opened the door to them, and saw the long, elegant black car parked at the curb in front of her house, she wished, for just a moment, that she could have seen the look on Constance Beckworth's face when the old woman first set eyes on it. Then she gave her whole and undivided attention to welcoming her tall, silver-haired, blue-eyed, aristocratic grandfather and her handsome, soon-to-be-brothers-in-law to Promise.

"Another beautiful granddaughter," Stuart said, his stern face brightening with a wide smile as he hugged her, then added with a quirk of his bushy eyebrows, "And unless I'm mistaken, a little great-grandchild on the way, too."

"Due at the end of September," Abby replied, taking him by the hand and leading him into the house after exchanging smiles with Sarah's fiancé, Ryan, and Jessica's fiancé, Sam.

Sam's daughters, Annie and Casey, Abby quickly discovered, had stayed in Willow Springs for the day under the watchful eye of Stuart's housekeeper.

Larissa's small house had never before been filled with so much laughter and noisy chatter as it was that Sunday. There were tears, too, but they were joyful tears, springing from the gratitude they all felt at finally being together.

As if conjured by a magician, the big, happy family Abby had always wanted now surrounded her, filling her with a sense of belonging unlike any she had ever known. And except for the time he spent alone with Stuart, discussing Deidre's condition, Jack was right there with her, too.

It was also Jack who, upon hearing her stomach growl shortly after noon, called the owner of the deli on the town square and organized a take-away meal to be picked up by the chauffeur that proved to be a big hit with everyone. In fact, Stuart was so impressed by the food that he talked about franchising the operation up in Willow Springs.

As the afternoon wore on, the men drifted into the living room to get to know each other better while the women sat around the kitchen table, nibbling on the last of the two dozen brownies Jack had so thoughtfully included in the deli order for dessert.

"So, it's settled, then," Jessica said, jotting down a note on the pad of paper in front of her. "Grandfather will send the jet for you, Hank and Judith, Jack and Jack's parents next Saturday, you'll all spend the night with us in Willow Springs and attend our first ever sisters' birthday party, stay another night, and fly home Monday morning."

"Sounds lovely," Abby murmured. "But are you sure you'll be able to pull everything together on your own in just six days?"

"Trust me…I grew up learning to entertain on short notice," Jessica replied, then ducked her head as a shadow of sadness flickered in her eyes.

"Deidre will be all right," Sarah said, reaching over to pat her hand.

"She doesn't have a right to be," Jessica murmured. "But she is my mother—the mother I knew, at least. And she isn't all bad."

"We know that," Abby assured her. "Just as we know Larissa wasn't all bad, either. They were just…misguided."

Obviously relieved by her sisters' understanding, Jessica brightened once again.

"Now for the next big event in our lives…" She pulled a day planner from her purse and flipped to the calendar for June. "I think we should plan a triple wedding for the third Saturday of the month in the garden at Grandfather's house."

"Oh, that would be so nice," Judith said, gazing at each of her granddaughters in turn, her eyes misting with tears.

Suddenly feeling uncomfortable, Abby sat back in her chair and began to twist her engagement ring round and round her finger.

"Better plan a double wedding, you two," she said, glancing first at Jessica, then at Sarah, before looking away self-consciously. "You see, Jack and I…we aren't really engaged. We're just…pretending. Because there was some gossip about me going around town and Jack wanted to protect me—"

"Just pretending?" Sarah's tone was so full of incredulity that Abby glanced at her again, startled. "You're kidding, aren't you?"

"She is," Jessica interjected, equally disbelieving. "She *has* to be."

"No, really…we *are*," Abby insisted. "Tell them, Gran."

"There's no pretending going on that I've seen," Judith stated unequivocally.

"Neither have I," Sarah said.

"Nor I," Jessica echoed as she reached across the table and took Abby's hand in hers. "Jack loves you and you love him. I've seen it in your eyes every time you look at each other. In fact, it's almost palpable every time you touch. Right, Sarah?"

"Exactly right."

"I admit I do love him," Abby said, looking down at the table. "But he doesn't love me. At least, he's never actually said he did."

"Probably because you've never given him a chance," Judith pointed out. "I know he hurt your feelings way back in December, but he's more than made up for it since then. Only you've been too stubborn to let yourself see it the way we all do."

"It's because of the baby," Abby protested, wanting to believe they were right about Jack, but still a little afraid to.

"Silly goose," Sarah sputtered in exasperation. "It's because of *you*. You're beautiful and sweet and kind and loving. Everything any man in his right mind would want in a wife."

"Yes, you most certainly are. And we should know," Jessica added with a smug smile. "Since you're just like us. Identical...in fact."

Abby couldn't help but laugh with her sisters, though tears blurred her eyes, as well. She was so lucky that they had found her, and so lucky they had opened their hearts to her, too.

They weren't stupid or silly, either. They were smart, savvy young women, and if they thought that Jack really loved her—

"Hey, what's going on in here?" Jack asked as he led the men into the kitchen.

"Just making plans," Jessica replied.

"Well, I hope you're just about finished," Stuart said. "I told the pilot to be ready to take us home no later than six o'clock tonight, so it's time for us to get on the road."

"Finished for now," Jessica told him with a wink at Abby. "We can pick up where we left off on Saturday. I'm sure you'll have everything sorted out by then, won't you, Abby?"

"One way or another," she answered in a wry tone that had her sisters grinning conspiratorially all over again.

After hugs and kisses all around, and a promise by Jessica to call so they could finalize the plans for their birthday party weekend, Stuart, Ryan and Sarah set off in the limousine with Sam and Jessica following in her rental car.

Back in the house, Abby filled a bag with some of the deli leftovers for Hank and Judith, then she and Jack took the obviously tired, but happy, couple back to their apartment.

"What a day," Hank said as he shook hands with Jack.

"A good day," Judith added, hugging Abby. "With many more to come. Our family certainly has grown."

"And it's going to grow even more." Hank winked at Abby.

"Oh, Granddad." She blushed as Jack put an arm around her shoulders.

"We'll talk tomorrow," Judith said. "Now you two run along and have some quiet time together."

On the short drive to her mother's house, Abby sat wordlessly, looking out the window, remembering what her sisters and her grandmother had said about Jack.

He, too seemed disinclined to talk, and when they pulled into the driveway, he hesitated before opening the car door.

"I can go on home if you would prefer to be by yourself tonight," he offered.

Abby looked over at him, wondering if that was what he wanted. He met her gaze steadily, but she couldn't really tell from his expression. In the past, she would have assumed that he'd had enough of her company for one day and told him to go.

But in the note he'd left for her he had said that there were things he needed to say, and he hadn't yet had the chance. If his sentiments were true and lasting, it wouldn't matter if he expressed them today, tomorrow, or the next day. Abby didn't want to wait, though.

She wanted Jack to say the words now—if such words were to be said—so she could start, immediately, to hold them close in her heart. And if he had no words for her, she wanted to know that, too.

She was tired of pretending. She wanted the real thing, she wanted it with Jack, and she wanted Jack to want it, too.

"Actually, I would rather be with you," she said, offering him a tentative smile.

His answering grin made her heart swell with hope.

"That's good because I wasn't really planning on leaving you here alone, anyway."

Jack got out of the car, walked around to the passenger side, opened the door with a flourish, and held out a hand to her. As Abby climbed out, then stood beside him, smoothing the skirt of her green knit dress, a garrulous voice hailed them from the yard next door.

"Quite a lot going on over there the past two days," Constance Beckworth stated. She stood on a patch of her lawn, her little dog cradled in her arms. "Thought I was seeing double."

"Triple," Jack told her. "You were seeing triple, or rather, triplets. Abby has two sisters. They came to Promise just to see her."

"Well, now, if that isn't a fine howdy-do. Three of you, huh? And limousines—two of them—one yesterday and an even bigger one today," Constance observed, her old eyes gleaming with curiosity. "What was that all about?"

"It's a long story," Abby said.

"One better left for another day," Jack added, scooping Abby into his arms and starting toward the front door.

"You young people...all you can think about is sex," the old woman grumbled.

Abby giggled as she clung to Jack, her arms around his neck.

"I'm thinking about something else," Jack murmured for her ears only.

"What's that?" Abby asked as he set her on her feet so she could unlock the door.

"Tell you when we're in the house."

"Okay, tell me," Abby insisted when they stood in the entryway with the door closed on Mrs. Beckworth's avid gaze. "What were you thinking about just now?"

"I'm not sure if I should. Every time I've tried in the past, you've cut me off. I've done my best to try to show you, too, but it hasn't seemed like you've been picking up my signals."

"I promise I'll listen to whatever you have to say without interrupting. As for your signals, I've been reading them loud and clear, only I've been afraid to admit it."

"Why is that, sweet Abby?" Jack asked, tracing the line of her jaw with his fingertips.

"Because I'd convinced myself that the message was too good to be true," she admitted, ducking her head.

"And now?"

"I don't want to pretend anymore. Jack?" Abby hesitated, then slanted her gaze at him again. "What about you?"

"Abby, my love, I was never pretending in the first place. Maybe just at the very outset. But that was really pretending to pretend so you wouldn't run away.

"I've loved you since that night we spent together in December and I will keep on loving you as long as there's breath in my body. That's why I asked you to marry me, and why I put a ring on your finger. And that's why I'll follow you wherever you want to go until eternity."

"Actually, I've come to like Promise quite a lot the past couple of weeks," she admitted with a shy smile.

"And me? Have you come to like me, too?"

"Oh, Jack, I've liked you as long as I can remember."

"Just…liked me?"

"Well, most of the time." She tilted her head to one side consideringly, then added, "As for the other—*loving* you—that never changed, and it never, ever, will."

Epilogue

Standing just outside the open French doors of the Walker mansion on the third Saturday in June, Abby looked out over the stone terraces and the gardens filled with flowers of every kind and color, her heart bursting with happiness.

Crowds of people, some she knew, others she would get to know, milled around the vast expanse of manicured lawn, the women looking lovely in their pastel summer dresses, the men sophisticated in their suits and ties.

By the buffet table, Jessica and her husband, Sam, helped his little daughters, Annie and Casey, choose from the wide selection of luscious food on offer.

Strolling hand-in-hand along a path winding through the beds of pink and pale yellow roses, Sarah and her husband, Ryan, paused, turned to each other and exchanged a long and tender kiss.

Hank and Judith, along with Elaine and J. B. Randall, sat at one of the white, linen-skirted tables, laughing heartily at something Stuart had just said.

Her family, all together on her wedding day, Abby thought, almost tempted to pinch herself to make sure she wasn't just dreaming.

How Jessica had managed to pull together such an elegant affair in only four weeks' time seemed like a miracle to Abby. Fortunately, Sarah had been able to help. With a resignation to tender and a town house to sell in San Francisco, Abby hadn't been able to do much except help to choose their dresses.

The three of them had fallen in love with the simple, sleeveless, ankle-length, ivory silk creation they had seen while shopping together in San Francisco, and that had been tailored just a little differently to suit each of their distinctive personalities. In lieu of a more traditional veil, they had also decided to wear small garlands of baby's breath woven in their hair.

The grooms, in their gray morning coats, were as handsome as their brides could have wanted. And Annie and Casey, doing the honors as flower girls, were exceptionally pretty in their long, pink-and-white striped dresses.

All in all, the day had been one of the best that Abby could remember. She was sorry that Larissa hadn't lived to see her reunited with her sisters. She knew, too, that Sarah missed her adoptive parents' presence, and that Jessica was burdened by Deidre's continued, and indefinite, confinement in a rest home.

But like the sun chasing away the shadows, their joy at finding each other, as well as the wonderful men they had chosen to marry, tempered their sadness.

Now, if only she could find her beloved—

"Ah, here you are," Jack said, coming up behind her and putting his arms around her. "I've been looking all over for you. Judith said you'd gone into the house, but with so many rooms, I felt like I was wandering around, lost in a maze."

"I'm glad you finally found me," Abby said, leaning back against him as he splayed a protective hand over her belly.

"Mmm, me, too…in more ways than one." He bent and kissed the side of her neck. "Having a good time, Mrs. Randall?"

"A wonderful time, Mr. Randall."

"Ready to join the party again?"

"In just a moment." Turning in her husband's arms, Abby put her hands on his shoulders and looked up at him. "I love you, Jack Randall."

"And I love you, sweet Abby…always and forever."

Holding her close, he kissed her, sealing his vow with a solemnity that made her dizzy with wonder and joy.

* * * * *

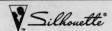

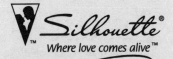

#1 *New York Times* bestselling author

NORA ROBERTS

brings you more of the loyal and loving,
tempestuous and tantalizing Stanislaski family.

Coming in February 2001

The Stanislaski Sisters

Natasha and Rachel

Though raised in the Old World traditions of their
family, fiery Natasha Stanislaski and cool, classy
Rachel Stanislaski are ready for a *new* world of love....

*And also available in February 2001 from
Silhouette Special Edition, the newest book in the
heartwarming Stanislaski saga*

CONSIDERING KATE

Natasha and Spencer Kimball's daughter Kate turns her
back on old dreams and returns to her hometown, where
she finds the *man* of her dreams.

Available at your favorite retail outlet.

Where love comes alive™

Coming soon from

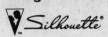

SPECIAL EDITION™

An exciting new miniseries
from bestselling author

SUSAN MALLERY

In the small town of
Lone Star Canyon, Texas,
the men are what fantasies
are made of—impossibly
handsome and rugged—
and the women are tempting
enough to melt their hearts.

Come visit Lone Star Canyon—where romance
and passion are as hot as the Texas sun!

THE RANCHER NEXT DOOR
(SE #1358, on sale November 2000)

UNEXPECTEDLY EXPECTING!
(SE #1370, on sale January 2001)

WIFE IN DISGUISE
(SE #1383 on sale March 2001)

Available at your favorite retail outlet.

Where love comes alive™

Don't miss this great offer to save on *New York Times* bestselling author Linda Howard's touching love story SARAH'S CHILD, a must have for any romance reader.

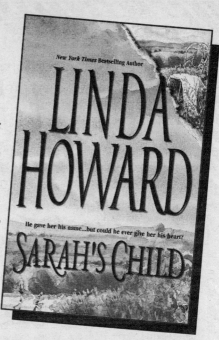

New York Times Bestselling Author

LINDA HOWARD

He gave her his name...but could he ever give her his heart?

SARAH'S CHILD

Available December 2000 wherever hardcovers are sold.

Don't miss this great offer to save on *New York Times* bestselling author Linda Howard's touching love story

SARAH'S CHILD, a must have for any romance reader.

New York Times Bestselling Author

LINDA HOWARD

He gave her his name...but could he ever give her his heart?

SARAH'S CHILD

Available December 2000 wherever hardcovers are sold.

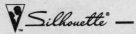

where love comes alive—online...

eHARLEQUIN.com

your romantic
books

- ♥ Shop online! Visit Shop eHarlequin and discover a wide selection of new releases and classic favorites at great discounted prices.

- ♥ Read our daily and weekly Internet exclusive serials, and participate in our interactive novel in the reading room.

- ♥ Ever dreamed of being a writer? Enter your chapter for a chance to become a featured author in our Writing Round Robin novel.

• • • • • •

your romantic
life

- ♥ Check out our feature articles on dating, flirting and other important romance topics and get your daily love dose with tips on how to keep the romance alive every day.

• • • • • •

your
community

- ♥ Have a Heart-to-Heart with other members about the latest books and meet your favorite authors.

- ♥ Discuss your romantic dilemma in the Tales from the Heart message board.

your romantic
escapes

- ♥ Learn what the stars have in store for you with our daily Passionscopes and weekly Erotiscopes.

- ♥ Get the latest scoop on your favorite royals in Royal Romance.

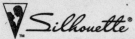

COMING NEXT MONTH

CMN1200